Keep Her

Keep Her

A NOVEL

by

LEORA KRYGIER

SHE WRITES PRESS

Published 2016
Printed in the United States of America
Print ISBN: 978-1-63152-143-0
E-ISBN: 978-1-63152-144-7
Library of Congress Control Number: 2016938931

For information, address:
She Writes Press
1563 Solano Ave #546
Berkeley, CA 94707

Cover design © Julie Metz, Ltd./metzdesign.com
Book design by Stacey Aaronson

She Writes Press is a division of SparkPoint Studio, LLC.

This is a work of fiction. Names, characters, places, and incidents either are the product of the author's imagination or are used fictitiously. Any resemblance to actual persons, living or dead, is entirely coincidental.

For Emma

It is a mild, mild wind

Moby Dick, Chapter 132

CHAPTER 1

H E WAS LOOKING AT ME.
No, more like staring at me—as open as the old camera he was holding, a camera with a big hole where the lens was supposed to be, and the insides exposed. And I stared right back at him, taking in all his colors.

Edges of sand-colored hair, soft, vein-blue eyes, and the green cover of the paperback book he was also holding.

I was fourth in line at the camera store, waiting to pick up some prints I'd ordered weeks ago, and before I knew it, I felt it coming on again, that same tug of war, the two sides of my overcrowded head going at it—numbers on the left, images and colors on the right, each trying to get my complete attention—when the two sides of my brain did something they never did. They called a fifteen-second truce and pounded out a strange joint mission in two short words, like an S.O.S.

Rescue.

Him.

"Hey, Aiden." A man I recognized as the owner of the shop, one of the last of the small camera stores left in the San Fernando Valley, appeared out of a back room and greeted him.

Aiden. I repeated the name to myself.

"Are we buying or selling today?" The owner said.

"Selling," Aiden said, his tall frame just a little bent over. "Wish I didn't have to." The camera was silver and black, and his fingers wrapped lovingly around the spot where the missing lens had once sat. He moved it gently across the counter toward the owner, the leather shoulder strap trailing behind.

"You sure you want to sell it? It's a rare model, you know," the owner asked.

"I know, my dad bought it in Japan. I just . . ."

"And what happened to the lens?"

"Lost it. Went overboard, actually. Can you believe it?" He shook his head. "My hands froze, I guess."

"Bad luck," the owner said, and Aiden nodded.

"I'll make out a check for you," I heard the owner say.

I looked up at the flat screen television above the counter. The weather guy on Channel 7 was going on about the heat wave, and the graphics below him pulsed across the screen.

Los Angeles, July 2009: One for the record books.

Froze? It was only the first week of July, but already the mercury hadn't budged from its mid-nineties spot, a killer heat mixed with Santa Ana winds. Even inside the store I could smell the stale smoke of the distant fires in the hills and canyons that surrounded the valley.

The television screen abruptly went black, and there was a weird quiet. One customer left and three people remained in line. Counting down. Numbers were good. They organized the world for me. My father, Miles, used to make my brother, Jordan, go along with me whenever I went outside to play. "Safety in numbers," Miles had cautioned. But I'd mixed it up. Somehow, I'd heard "Safety is numbers," and that's how it stayed, fixed in my mind—that numbers would always be safe. But my right brain disagreed now, as usual, and nudged me to pull out my camera.

Snap a random photograph.

"Eww, terrible," someone a few feet ahead of me said, then took out some photos from a canary yellow Kodak envelope. She held the photos up to the ceiling light and inspected them. I could see that the photos were mostly dark and grainy, amateur attempts and flash failures, mistakes. "C-ra-ppy, aren't they?" the girl said to the person standing next to her in line.

Suddenly the girl's voice and stick-straight hair were completely familiar. It sounded exactly like my best friend, even though she'd been MIA for a couple of months now.

I edged up to get a closer look. "Bryn?"

"Yes. It's me, Maddie." She turned and said my name, loud. "This is kizzz-mit," Bryn exclaimed, and she turned again, this time toward Aiden. In the corner, I saw Aiden tilting his head just slightly in our direction, a movement so tiny, almost indiscernible, but I could tell he was listening to what we were saying.

"What is?"

"Us bumping into each other, of course." I'd met Bryn the summer my parents had sent me to a horseback riding camp in Ojai. Bryn's mother had also coerced her into going, and we gravitated toward each other, the only two non-equestrians, both choking with laughter when we lagged behind all the other girls on the horse trails, and we'd been friends ever since, but I hadn't seen her in a long time. "Definitely kizzz-mit." She repeated. She was always looking up the origin of words and names and had a theory that people lived up to the meaning of their names, but kismet was more than just a word for Bryn.

"Sure, I remember. Kismet. There are no accidents, no coincidences, just the very powerful hand of fate, right?" She'd also told me that the origin of the word was the Arabic word *qisma*.

Bryn frowned. "You can joke about it all you want, but–" She glanced at Aiden again. Bryn looked exactly the same, her long blonde hair flat-ironed, her purple bra showing beneath her spaghetti-strap camisole. Her voice was husky, almost hoarse, a little like one of the Power Bars she was always munching on, salty-sweet. Only her face was thinner, the mascara in clumps on her lower lashes. But she looked at me closely and broke out in a smile. "I see you're wearing the pomegranate T-shirt I gave you, the one I brought for you from that London museum my mom dragged me to." The shirt was a little faded from washings, but the print, a graphic reproduction of an old, botanical illustration, was still bright, a pomegranate hanging from its stem, along with a cross-section of the fruit, exposing the ruby-red seeds.

I smoothed down the sides of the shirt and felt the soft bottom between my fingertips. I glanced over at Aiden, who was looking at me again. Pale, he looked like he'd seen a ghost.

"It's still my favorite."

"That's good. Ver-ry good."

"And you know, your photos aren't as bad as you think."

"No, no. They're definitely path-etic," she said, and then tried to stuff them back in the envelope, but the envelope didn't cooperate, so she crammed the photos into her bag.

"Let me see them?" I asked, and Bryn retrieved the photos from the bag. They were now slightly bent from the pressure of her fingertips. "I could do something with them."

She thought a minute, and her expression changed. "Do something with them? Oh, your *collages*. I forgot," she said.

"But I haven't been able to make a single piece . . . in a long time."

Bryn narrowed her eyes at me. "Since Jordan messed up again, right?"

"You know me too well."

"Here." She chose one of the photos, and handed it to me. "You have it. It's just one less for me to tear up and throw away," she laughed, but then she lowered her voice. "What about your brother? What's going on?"

"He has another court date tomorrow morning, and we all have to be there. Oh, and he calls himself Jorge these days."

"Jorge? I'm sorry, Maddie," Bryn said, reaching out to touch my hand, and when she did, I thought I heard the sound of water running somewhere. It was a peaceful sound, so soft, yet somehow it made me uneasy.

Bryn got a text. "My mom, again. Sorry. I have to go." She ran out past Aiden. The camera body that had hung from his shoulder was missing now, and he seemed a little lost without it. He was closer to me by now and I realized I'd been wrong about his eyes. There were over four hundred variations of blue on the Pantone color chart, and now his eyes seemed grayer to me, a vapor-blue.

"What can I do for you?" a woman behind the counter asked me, loudly, as though it was the second time she'd asked.

My head snapped back to her. I had to forget about Bryn, about Jordan's latest crash and burn, and about him, Aiden. "I'm picking up some special order photos."

While the woman rifled through a box of envelopes behind the counter, I retrieved the photo I'd taken earlier on my camera, waiting in line. It was a lopsided photo, just a customer's floating torso, off-center to the ceiling, but I liked the asymmetrical point of view.

The woman looked up from the box. "Sorry, it's not here. But don't worry, I'll call the lab."

I tried to peek into her box. "You sure it's not lost?"

"Happens a lot, lately," she grumbled. "I promise I'll call you."

"Okay, call me," I said, and I turned to leave when Bryn suddenly reappeared.

"I was thinking about what you said before, about your collages . . . and . . . you could have some more of my rejects, if you want."

I saw an instant replay of Bryn's photos in my head, the jackpot of odd images I could cut up and then connect with other found objects. "That would be great."

"They're no good to me," Bryn said. "You know, actually, take them all," she groaned, leafing through the photos one at a time, as though she was saying good-bye not only to them, but also to me. "So, how's it feel?" Bryn asked, unscrewing the top of her lip gloss and dabbing her bottom lip. "To be done with high school?" She looked at me and narrowed her eyes. "Completely done," she sighed. "And a year earlier than the rest of us on top of that. I wish my mom had just let me take a GED test, like you did. Lucky you," she sighed again.

"Lucky?" I told her that my father was still not on board about the New York art school thing. And there was the money problem. Jordan's newest private lawyer was costing my parents big time. I was sure they were digging into their savings. She looked sympathetic, and the Bryn-less months were momentarily erased. "It didn't exactly add up when I applied to art school. I can't even draw. It was a very un-Maddie impulse."

"No it wasn't," Bryn declared with certainty. "It wasn't an impulse. It was supposed to happen."

"There you go again."

I stole another quick glance at Aiden. His gaze was still steady on me. He looked just a little older than Jordan. Twenty-one? That would make him barely four years older than me. His lashes were long and dark, but his beauty wasn't simple, as though he was the trick answer to a multiple-choice question on a math test, none of the above. I forgot about Bryn and began to march right over toward him.

But before I reached him I felt a vibration, the store windows starting to rattle and then violently shake. What sounded like a thunderclap followed and there was the roar of a fast gush of water at my feet. In a second, water was everywhere, rising quickly and more than a foot high, and the current almost knocked me right off my feet.

"Get out, get out!" someone yelled. "It looks like a water main outside! It's coming in!" someone else shouted as the rush of water rose.

Everyone in the store began to grab whatever they could and headed for the door.

"We have to get out of here," Bryn cried. "Let's go,

let's go, Maddie!" she yelled, just as another torrent of water came rushing at us. This time the deluge had a muddy, oily-slick coating.

I saw it as it happened, like a memory and a premonition all at once, the scene in a sequence, snipped and disassembled into pieces. A whirlpool of water found its way to Bryn's heels, then her sandals separated from the floor, the water ripping them off her feet.

I lunged toward Bryn, but Aiden was quicker and more precise. One of his hands took hold of her wrist, while the other searched for her elbow. I saw her sliding away from his grip, but he held on tighter and Bryn was able to steady herself on the counter.

"Thank you. Thank you," she called out to Aiden, breathing hard.

Suddenly, the room seemed to move around me, and I thought I was slipping too, but Aiden grabbed me just as I was about to fall backwards.

By this time, everyone else had gone. The lights sputtered and then went out completely, and I could only see the outline of Aiden's body like a charcoal sketch.

"Come on, Maddie," Bryn implored, as she ran out the door, but suddenly I couldn't move.

Several moments ticked by, and the distant sirens began to get closer. I started to walk to the door, but it was as if I was walking in slow motion. There were molecules shifting and doubling, and an impossible, implausible pang ran like electricity down my body.

Then a group of firemen sprinted inside in a blur of bulky jackets and strips of yellow reflective tape stretched across their chests. They carried long pike poles and water pumps.

Get out. Get out.

"You have to leave. It's not safe," one of the firemen yelled at me, wildly pointing to the large hole where water, mixed with chunks of concrete, had blown in through a wall.

Through the cracked store window I could now see the powerful geyser of water outside on the street, shooting upwards almost four stories into the air, but I still couldn't get my feet to take a step.

The water was white-cold.

But somehow it didn't feel dangerous, like the time it had suddenly rained on my parents' backyard Fourth of July barbecue. It almost never rained in California in July, and we'd all stood there, wet and happy with disbelief. I'd been the first to take off my shoes and jump into the puddles. My younger sister, Gabriela, then Jordan and Bryn followed my example, and then even my father and mother, Leah. It was the last time I remembered everyone being in sync, our backyard shiny with water.

"You two have to leave!" the same fireman yelled again. "Damned old cast-iron water pipes," he reported into a walkie-talkie. "Third one this month," he said. "Must be a thirty-incher this time."

"Come," Aiden urged me. He was so close to me I

could see his heartbeat pulsing in his neck. "Come, Maddie," he said. His voice was quiet and calm, and I was surprised I could hear him over the din of water and trucks and people yelling. He took hold of my hand, and, as though I was in a time warp, suddenly I was outside, just as more fire engines came screeching to a halt. The water was mud-brown at my ankles and the geyser was still gushing, the asphalt ripped open and collapsed. More firemen appeared and yelled at us, this time to get off the sidewalk in front of the store.

My pomegranate T-shirt was partly wet but strangely silky on my skin. I looked around for Bryn, but she was nowhere in sight. I looked behind me. It had only been minutes since the first gush of water, but everything had definitely been reshuffled.

"Here," Aiden said, handing me something. It was Bryn's photographs, sopping wet, and a little bent and blurry now. "You dropped these in there. But the photos aren't ruined. I think you can still use them."

I looked at the photographs then looked at him carefully. "How did you know? How in the world would you know that?"

He only shrugged, but he was exactly right. The photos weren't ruined at all. They were perfect.

CHAPTER 2

B Y NOW A BIG CROWD HAD GATHERED AND A string of news vans and water department trucks was pulling up from all directions. I scanned the crowd again for Bryn, but she'd disappeared. I was still a little shaky and cold, and Aiden put his arm around me and walked me across the street where we sat side by side on a low wall directly across from the store, trying to warm up in the sun. The geyser of water was still going, and one of the fire captains came by and told us the water had to be shut off gradually so as not to create pressure surges and ruptures in other pipes. Water hammers, he called it. I looked out at the trail of mud, broken glass, sandbags and debris everywhere.

Stuck there, we waited for the firemen to secure the area before they would let us get to our cars. Meanwhile, someone brought out some clean towels to wipe off our feet. Someone else handed out bottled waters. I tried to call Bryn but there was no answer.

"You okay?" Aiden asked.

I looked down at my Converse, still soaking wet, but the hot sun felt good on my neck. "I think so." Across the street, the firemen were mopping up. "Those guys—they were pretty amazing," I said. "And you too. You knew exactly what to do."

"Hey, what I did . . . there's no comparisons to those firefighters."

"Maybe . . . but still . . . really impressive."

He smiled, then reached over, and plucked out a tiny leaf that had settled in the curly ends of my dark hair.

"Here," he said, handing the leaf to me just as a fireman announced the all-clear, and we got up and started to walk toward the lot behind the camera store where our cars were parked.

When we reached our cars, we looked at each other and laughed.

"What are the chances that our cars are parked right next to each other?" he asked.

I looked over at the number of parking spaces reserved for the camera store, and quickly calculated. "One out of five?"

He laughed, and looked at his watch. "I'm hungry. You?"

"Actually, I'm starving.

"How about we get away from this mess?" he suggested "The Galleria has a bunch of restaurants and cafes."

I hesitated.

"It's not that far. I'll follow you."

"Well, okay," and we decided to meet up near the outdoor fountain. But I'd only driven two blocks when the used car my parents had given me for my birthday stalled. I peered up at my rear view mirror and saw that Aiden was right behind me, and somehow, my car sputtered back to life. I got to the mall parking structure but lost sight of his car in the multi-tiered lot. As soon as I got out of my car, I tried calling Bryn again to see if she was okay, but her phone went immediately to voicemail. By the time I'd walked through the low-slung lot and up the half-escalator, it felt like I'd walked three long blocks. My mother once told me that in the eighties the mall had been a closed box, completely indoors, but it had been torn down and divided into two open-air swaths of small stores, restaurants, multi-plex movie theaters and a gym that all formed a wind tunnel.

The stairs didn't seem to end. Stadium seating movie theaters sat atop three escalators that overlooked the intersecting 405 and 101 freeways, and after the second escalator I had a funny sensation, a complete feeling of imbalance, as though I was being pulled in by a magnet, but I didn't know whether it was pulling me up or down.

Aiden was exactly where he said he would be, on a bench near the fountain. He couldn't have been more than a few minutes ahead of me, but he looked like a still life, completely settled into the bench and absorbed by the book that sat in his lap. There was something else too, besides the yellow Post-it notes that peeked out of his book, a phone, which he kept checking then putting back in his pants pocket. When he saw me, he put the book and the phone away, leaned back, clasped his hands behind his head, and smiled. "I put down our names for a table, but it's a twenty-minute wait."

"That's okay." I said, and sat down. I was about to say something else when I looked down and noticed an old bottle cap embedded in the checkerboard tile under his feet. It seemed out of place in the expanse of perfect tiles, as if someone had rooted it there on purpose, to leave a mark.

"Maybe it's a leftover from *Fast Times*," Aiden said, as if he'd heard the question in my head.

"From what?"

"*Fast Times at Ridgemont High*, you know, the cult classic. It was filmed here."

"Oh." I had a vague recollection of Leah mentioning that movie, too. "Just so you know," I started. "I was born in Guatemala. My parents flew down to Guatemala three times to adopt babies. My older brother, Jordan was first, then me, and last, Gabriela."

He looked amused. "Oh. I see. Well okay, then," he replied, smiling. "I see you like to get things out of the way, and right off. That's good. Did you always know you were adopted?"

"All three of us knew early on. My mom is one of those no-secrets-in-this-family kind of person, and I know the names of my birthparents, the name of their village, even the names of their other children. In any case, there was no way my parents could have kept it a secret. We don't look anything like them."

"So, I guess you speak Spanish?" he asked.

"Not really. My mom tried to convince me to take Spanish back in third grade, part of her raising-your-adopted-children-and-keeping-their-cultural-heritage mandate, but that didn't work for me."

He smiled. "Anything else you want to tell me?'

I looked at him and a crazy feeling came over me. It was crazy and sudden, but it was there. I saw us together, like two accidental pieces that came together in a collage, and I had to tell him now, right off. "There is something else. My brother. He's in trouble. He's done some stupid things, and . . . I'm not really sure what's going to happen to him," I said, waiting for him to flinch with the information. But he didn't.

"It's okay. I understand," he said.

"You do? So, now it's your turn. What about you, besides you being a film buff?"

He was a film major at UCLA, he said, but he was taking a leave of absence to work on a short subject documentary. "I'm staying with an old Navy buddy of my dad's, and working night shifts logging in videotapes for a TV show," he said. "And by the way, just so you know, I was born down near Redondo Beach," he said, the edges of his mouth crinkling up in a wider smile. "But I think we should move. I'm broiling and I think it's cooler over there," he continued, pointing to another bench closer to the fountain. "I'll go get us some cold drinks before lunch, and before we both melt out here."

We both got up, but the fountain caught my eye. It was surrounded by tall streetlamps, and had three, round tiers, like a wedding cake, the first low tier bubbling up, then the second and third joined. I moved in closer, standing up on the narrow rim. It was wetter than I expected, and I slipped just a little on the edge, my feet traveling from under me, just about to fall. From the corner of my eye I saw Aiden run toward me, but I regained my equilibrium just as he sprinted over.

"I think we've had enough falling for one day," he said, catching his breath. "Don't you know that standing on the edge of fountains can be dangerous?" he asked, grinning widely, and I could now see he had just the tiniest space between his two very white front teeth. "I would have caught you again, you know . . . if you'd given me the chance."

Suddenly there was a pounding in my ears, a vacuum of space and air, and it took all my concentration just to stand up straight. "You know, I'm not feeling so well. This is weird, but I'm a little dizzy. I think I should go," I said, making a move to leave.

"You okay? Should I drive you home?"

"No, I'm all right, really." But the water rushing into the store was now replaying on a crazy loop in my head.

"Are you sure? You look a little green."

"No, I'm good," I said, my head still swimming.

"If we weren't on solid ground, I'd say you're looking seasick."

"Seasick? That's kind of ridiculous." But I was beginning to think he might be right.

"Hey, there's no shame in that. I spent an entire week seasick on a ship . . . once."

"You did? On a ship?"

"I eventually I got over it. It was only a year and a half ago." He closed his eyes and paused for a split second. "But now it seems like a million years ago," he said then stopped abruptly. "I think you should at least let me walk you to your car," he said, and I was thankful he was beside me when we walked back to the parking structure through the windy path.

"I know this is completely awkward, but before you go . . ." he paused, then continued. "You shouldn't be the only one to get things out of the way."

"Get what out of the way?" I asked.

"I'll tell you my worst three traits," he said, flashing a smile. "And then it will be as if you've always known me."

"What?"

"One. Sometimes I can be a little OCD, and sometimes not at all. Two. I'm often self-conscious, and easily distracted. Three. I tend to overanalyze. Everything. And actually, in all fairness, I should also tell you that I screw up. A lot."

"Funny," I managed to sputter out. "And is there anything else you want to tell me?"

"Oh lots," he laughed, but his face clouded over, just a bit. "But we can leave that all for tomorrow. Tomorrow afternoon," he said.

"Tomorrow?" I repeated, a little confused.

"It's all very clear to me now . . . the camera store, plus the water, plus your friend. It all equals meant-to-be."

I laughed. "You know that that's not a real mathematical equation."

"You have to promise me you'll meet me again tomorrow," he continued, with a look that made me feel as though he was the one who had made some other pledge. "Promise?"

"Sure," I said, but I was anything but sure.

"I know what you're thinking," he said. "I didn't always believe in all that stuff either." And looking at him, the way his body arced toward me just slightly, his sweet face, all I wanted was to believe in his meant-to-be. He gave me his phone number and told me where he'd be and what time, and I promised.

On the way back to my car, I squinted in the bright sun as we walked toward the escalator. Aiden was just behind me, like an anchor holding me upright, but as I grabbed onto the moving banister I had the same sensation as before, a pull of gravity, and it seemed as though it was coming from all sides rather than below.

I couldn't tell whether I was falling down or falling up, but of one thing I was completely certain.

I was falling.

September 20, 2007

Dear Alex—

I can't believe it's been six years since the accident. But it seems right that we begin today, just a few days before what would have been your eighteenth birthday. It's the start for both of us, even though you're not here, even though you're gone. I hate that word, gone. It's just another one of those stupid things people say, like passed-away, departed, left us, all those words people use instead of saying it—that you died, that you're dead.

The mission, our mission, begins today, even though we aren't scheduled to sail for two months and I'm trying so hard to be more like you, and even though I know I'm only a poor substitute, a lousy stand-in for you, and for what you would have become. First thing when I got off the bus from Atlanta, they handed me a sign-in sheet, and I wrote down my name, Aiden Ross. But it should have been you, little brother. It should have been your name on that sign-in sheet, Alex Robert Ross.

It's the last days of summer, but you wouldn't know it. It's still hot and humid here in the South, 96 degrees Fahrenheit and 89 percent humidity. I want to write down as many facts, figures too, as I possibly can for you, because I know you. You would want to know every detail. You used to say that it's the little parts of things that are important, the small pieces that make up a whole, so I'll try to tell you as much as I can, and it'll be as if you're with me here. And speaking of little things, I'm sorry this letter is so messy. I just ripped this out of an old film production workbook that I had, stains and all. I'm trying to take as little with me as possible, and so whatever I find on the way, I'll use to write to you.

A cloudy sky bears down on us with faint bolts of lightning in the distance. It's my first time in a southern state and there's a heavy, buggy thickness in the air. The sky draws everything down with it, along with the Spanish moss that drips down from the trees.

We're camped out in tents for an NVDA, the acronym for non-violent direct action, three-day basic training. We're four to a tent, randomly grouped. First are the hours of classes, which include some history, collaboration techniques, organizational skills, tactics and team building. We sit around and role-play and discuss possible scenarios, and by the afternoon the blackboard is completely full of words and timelines, the white chalk overtaking the black.

At the very end of the day, the instructor takes a few of us aside and shows us his own logbook from an earlier mission. The columns spread neatly across the ledger-like paper, detailing dates and times, longitudes and latitudes, ocean depths, currents, wind direction and velocity, and cloud types. It contains an exact recollection of the details, and I take the empty, leftover, columned pages the instructor offers me. It's 9:00 p.m. now, and there's a wind coming from the south, southwest, SSW.

Night falls slowly in the South, and in my tent someone pulls out a laptop and sets up a ship simulator video game. I watch for a bit as he controls the variables like wave height, speed, and weather. He steers a virtual speedboat between ships, leaning left and right, and my hands begin to tremble uncontrollably. He turns around to me and asks. Hey, Aiden, you want a turn on this? I can't even manage to tell him no. I haven't touched a video game since the accident. But I can only shake my head, and I have to leave the tent to breathe. Outside, the air is danker than in the tent.

On the second day, we're led outside. We learn to put ourselves in arm tubes that can be used to form a human chain and block off an entrance or a road, and we're taught how to climb up ropes in harnesses. This, so we can scale buildings, and then bring ourselves back down on a banner drop. There's scaffolding all around the forty-foot training structure. It takes me hours to master the multi colored ropes and the karabiner link, an oblong metal link with one spring hinged side, along with a pulley, and get an understanding of how each slides and interacts with each other. Even the simple helmet takes some getting used to, this feeling of enclosure against my head.

On the last day there's basic seamanship and boat handling. We all wear life jackets and learn to tie nautical knots. The main goal is for each one of us to know how to handle a speedboat, especially in a choppy ocean, and we all take turns at the steering wheel. This part of the training is easiest for me. After all, the ocean is in our blood. Still, I wonder how I'll meet the next challenge.

Al—ways —
Aiden

October 11, 2007

Dear Alex—

London is where I'm taking an advanced climb training. I
have three days to kill before we start and I spend a couple
of rainy days holed up in a cramped hostel on the edge of
London, but it's good. It gives me a lot of time to think,
something I've been so carefully avoiding for a very long
time. One afternoon, the rain finally lets up and I walk
the city for hours, following the crooked path of the
Thames, past the London Eye and the Houses of
Parliament. I take out the old Nikkormat camera Dad
gave me and take a few photos of the barges gliding on the
river. The soft, insistent lap of the water reminds me of
you. That second night in the hostel I have so many
dreams, but I can't remember any of them, except one. It's
about a girl, a dark-haired girl.

The next day I head out to the river again, but this
time with the other trainees. Our first challenge is to climb
an unused crane on the river. After being dropped off by a
speedboat, we climb up the ladder and steps to where the
operator used to sit. Then we climb up one of the four
metal poles that project up from the crane. We put straps
around the pole, clip onto the first one then position the
second. I shift my weight over and then move again,
repeating this again and again, soon exhausted by having
to heave myself just inches at a time, while the harness cuts
into my legs. There's also the height to get used to, and the
thought of falling down onto the hard wooden jetty below
as the crane shudders and bounces with my every move.

Coming down is almost worse. My knees are shaking long before we reach bottom.

What looks like a police van is waiting for us on the jetty. It's dark now, and the police lights they aim at us are blinding, and the sirens piercing.

Get down. Get down. Step away from the jetty. Put your hands behind your head, the bullhorn commands us. And even though it's just an exercise, a sham detention, I feel what it's like to be handcuffed, the cold metal hard and unforgiving around my wrists. I feel what it's like to be pulled into a vehicle, head down and later, yanked out by the elbow with my hands tied tight behind my back. In fourteen days, I'll be on a plane to the Netherlands.

> *Al - ways -*
> *Aiden*

November 2, 2007

Dear Alex—

Amsterdam is full of bikes, even at 2:00 a.m. Wherever I look, it's a city on two-wheels. There are masses of bikes, some parked and stationary in huge bike lots, and the rest moving, almost in unison, through the city, their spokes flying. Most of the trainees spend a few days in Amsterdam, walking the canals and visiting the museums, but I can't get away from the bikes and Amsterdam fast enough. It's too much of a reminder. I take the first train out from the Centraal Station, a nineteenth-century rail station that sits in front of the harbor, to Den Helder, the last Dutch port before entering the North Sea. Den Helder is a small town on the tip of a lowland peninsula and its port berths naval ships, submarines, and tall sailing ships of the past. An old Napoleonic fortress and a bright red lighthouse stand out from the landscape like words of caution, but I think of you, and ignore their warnings.

I'm in a cheap hotel not far from the railway station. The hotel, known mostly for its rowdy bar, is where sailors and townspeople come to soak up the local beer, play pool and darts. I try my luck at darts, but I never quite hit the bull's-eye. Out in the night air, it's cold but I walk to the lighthouse and to the fortress and back. When I return to the hotel, I can't sleep.

The next day I meet up with the twelve other trainees for onboard training, the last hurdle for new, ship-based action volunteers. On board, I realize I have some sailing skills already, thanks to Dad's friend Jack. I know my way around the rounded hatches of a ship. I know the difference between port and starboard, and even how to spell phonetically so I can be understood on the ship's radio. I know that 1 knot equals 1.15 miles or 6,076 feet per hour. But somehow, I know I shouldn't let this lull me into a false sense of security.

Pretty soon the real training begins, and it's hell. The trainers orchestrate scenarios in blocks of thirty-six hours. They recreate situations for us to overcome in very compressed timelines. There are equipment failures, false alarms, dead camera batteries, toxic waste on the deck, all engineered glitches to test us, strain us, as we make stupid, sleep-deprived decisions on how to react and respond.

We learn to question everything and to sift out the real emergencies from the fake ones they devise for us. We learn how to make backup plans and contingencies without working Internet. We learn to deal with our inevitable mistakes. Curve ball after curve ball is fired at us, including phony troublemakers, all so we can be ready for the real thing ahead. Trainees get pissed and tempers flare up. But I know that even after overcoming anger and the pressure of living in close quarters, luck and weather can still easily conspire against us and undo all our months of solid preparation.

I'm shivering. The dry suit my trainer picked out for me before climbing up the boarding ladder isn't dry. I should have inspected it myself and not relied on my trainer. I should have understood that this was another test of my resolve and decision-making, but I didn't.

I'm wet through and through, shaking. My fingers freeze on the edge of a six-by-six foot banner and I try, with all my last reserves, to hang it on the side of a moving ship, and to keep my promise to you.

Al - ways -
Aiden

CHAPTER 3

I WOKE UP AND REMEMBERED HOW AIDEN HAD SAID the word "to-morrow" with a little pause, like it was a New Year's toast. I'd heard Leah say that "tomorrow" was the most hopeful word in the English language, and for once I agreed with my mother. My bedroom was a little cooler in the early morning, a tiny breeze sending the curtains fluttering. The curtains were the only evidence of Leah's handiwork in my room, though. I liked to keep my worktable neat, all my art supplies and camera books and equipment lined up in a tall, open cabinet. And on two of my walls I'd pinned the old, large-scale drawings of airplane designs Miles had drafted in his MIT days.

I dressed, then texted Bryn to see how she was doing, but she still didn't respond. Leah called from the kitchen, but on my way out of my bedroom I noticed that a tube of watercolor, my favorite, cadmium yellow, had fallen to the floor, and I stopped to pick it up, opened the tube and smudged a bit of the paint between my fingers.

Purest of colors, yellow reflects the most light.

Like the reflective tape on the firefighters' jackets.

I decided not to wash it off, to let it sink into my fingertips.

I smiled to myself as I came down the stairs and into the kitchen. The little thirteen-inch TV was, as usual, tuned to the local news station, but fixed on mute and closed-captioned. I leaned on the counter, trying to fan myself with the paint sample brochures Leah had left on the table. The kitchen was an ever-changing project for my mother. Only three months ago she'd painted the aging wood cabinets a tacky shade of tropical aqua to match the border of Spanish tile, and had changed all the cabinet hardware to little pulls and knobs shaped like forks and spoons, but she was already planning to repaint.

Then I remembered. We all had to go to court.

"Hungry?" Leah asked, and pointed to the eggs and hash browns she'd just made on the stove. My mother rarely made breakfast, but there was always a mega meal for everyone the mornings of Jordan's court hearings, even her heart-shaped blueberry pancakes, but the unspoken deal was that no one talked about Jordan or lawyers or court.

"So, what did Jordan's lawyer say exactly about his chances?" I asked, and my mother shot me a look. My stomach was queasy, but the eggs looked good this morning, sunny-side up and crispy. I grabbed a plate, wolfing them down. Leah opened the kitchen window with a view of our dying lawn and sighed, then gathered up the bottles and cans from the recycling bins she'd recently installed underneath the kitchen sink. She didn't answer my question.

Miles looked up from his tablet. Even though he'd been laid off from Boeing where he worked as an engineer four years ago, my father was still as precise and logical as the Boeing logo—a thin line rendering of a planet, an orbital swoosh, and the hint of jet wings on a horizon.

"Did you know that water mains have been breaking all over the city?" Miles asked me. "A thirty-inch pipe can spew out over 30,000 gallons of water a minute," he mused. "Did you know that even in as little as six inches of moving water, a person can lose their footing? I heard there was a break in the East Valley yesterday, near that camera store you go to."

"Oh, really?" I said, looking down at my plate. I was sure that telling them I was there would have led to too many questions.

"It's those new restrictions about watering only on certain days, because of the drought. There was an overload of water usage," Leah piped in.

"It's climate change. The oceans warming up," Miles said, shaking his head. "Right, Maddie?" He stood up to give me a hug, and his tan jacket smelled lemony.

"Sure, sure, Dad," I said, but I was already thinking about Jordan, locked up in Juvenile Hall on a third offense.

Leah called out to Gabriela, who was still upstairs, and she came down and we all got into the car.

"It's just a mistake, a misunderstanding," Leah said, when we got to the freeway.

I shook my head. "Come on, Mom. You know there was no *mistake* or misunderstanding." The warehouse had been vandalized with slap tags, large stickers that taggers pre-mark with gang graffiti and slap on quickly. They were the same exact brand of cheap labels my dad sold at his mailbox store. And the handwriting was Jordan's brand of graffiti block letters, topped off with the special "i" he always dotted with the number eight, rotated to the side, at 90 degrees, an infinity symbol.

Above us a half-dozen helicopters flew in the direction of the fires in the north, and I wished I'd thought of driving separately, in my own car. But I wasn't thinking straight. It felt like the heat and the ochre haze of smoke and dark plumes in the distance were trapped in my head.

"The lawyer said we have to show the judge we're a *strong family*," Miles said, turning around to me. His voice was calm, but his lower lip trembled just a little, and I saw the effort it took for him to engineer the strength he needed to say those two simple words, "strong family."

"We all have to rally around him," he continued, but suddenly Leah hit the brakes as the car ahead stopped short, its tires screeching.

Leah's right hand flew reflexively across the passenger seat then she smacked both hands down on the steering wheel. "He can't go back to jail," she cried out. "And we have to do everything we possibly can to make sure he doesn't."

Next to me, Gabriela started to cry, and I put my arm around her and held her close to me. My sister's face was long and thin, like Jordan's, and her slender body was hardly a sliver of flesh. She'd just turned thirteen.

"It's okay. He will be okay." I said, trying hard to echo Miles, to be more like my father, but my heart was pounding.

It was a couple of weeks past the longest day of the year, daylight losing about a minute a day, but it didn't feel like the days were getting any shorter with a heat that wouldn't quit.

I tried to open the window, but I'd forgotten that Leah's back seat window was broken, stuck shut. There were tiny beads of sweat forming above my upper lip. My hair, already damp, was sticking to the back of my neck. I closed my eyes, but I could see the route in my head— the 405, to Interstate 5, then eastward to the 210. After the exit, there would be low industrial buildings, followed by yards of barbed wire scraping the tops of the walls of the juvenile hall compound. It would lead directly into the concrete block courthouse that sat in a no-man's land in the northeastern part of the San Fernando Valley.

Leah stopped at a Seven-Eleven to get a Slurpee for Jordan, his favorite.

"Really, Mom?" I said when she came out with the

brightly colored paper cup. "I don't think the sheriff is going to let you give him that in the courtroom."

"Never mind," she said, handing the drink to my dad to hold.

Later, Leah parked the car and we all filed through the metal detectors at the entrance to the courthouse. Leah's oversized tote bag got stuck in the X-Ray machine and Miles emptied out his pants' pockets clumsily, his change clattering to the cement floor. People grumbled behind us.

Jordan's lawyer met us in the packed waiting room. She was tall, with shoulder-length hair and a cropped blue blazer that matched her clipped, half-sentence explanation. We all sat down and Miles and Leah huddled to talk strategy with her, while Gabriela rested her head on my lap.

An hour later we all moved to the back of a windowless courtroom and Jordan appeared from lockup through a metal side door. I couldn't exactly see what happened, but there was a noisy scuffle at the door. Leah almost bolted up from her chair then we all heard the deputy telling Jordan to calm down.

"All good, man," Jordan said, shaking the deputy's large hand off his shoulder. Then he swaggered in, wearing juvenile hall-issue grey sweatshirt and sweatpants, the bottom of his too-big pants bunching up at his shoes. Slight, Jordan looked a lot younger than his age, which was a month shy of eighteen, but all I could see were the little parts of him, his hard eyes, almost metallic, and his newest tattoos, teardrops on his knuckles, in darkest, indigo blue.

The beat-up chairs in the back of the courtroom were all mismatched, a jumbled line of office and secretarial chairs, along with some old wooden chairs from other eras, and I ran my hand over my wooden armrest, carved up with etchings. The room was quiet, when suddenly there was movement around the judge's bench—clerks, probation officers, and counselors going back and forth with thick case files.

It didn't look like it was going too well for Jordan. The judge, Jordan's attorney, and the DA argued back and forth for a long time. The DA brought up each and every one of Jordan's priors, and I thought Leah would faint dead away at the list of all his other offenses.

I held my breath while Jordan signed a plea bargain along with a long list of conditions of his probation, which the judge read out loud, one by one. Jordan would be released, but would have to live in a court-ordered placement.

Jordan smiled, and when he saw Miles leaning forward, zeroed in on him, he gave him his widest grin. For once, Jordan was getting exactly what he always wanted—Miles's full and undivided attention.

"Please, don't blow this," I mouthed to Jordan.

Please, not this time.

"Partly cloudy, but no rain in the thirty-day forecast," he answered me, but he wasn't smiling anymore.

It was part of the game we used to play, mimicking the blonde weather girl on the Channel 4, 11:00 p.m. local news, a private joke between us, just before we went to bed, but it made no sense for him to say it now.

Later, when we arrived back at the parking lot, Miles realized he'd forgotten Jordan's drink in the car. In the heat, it had become a cloudy swirl of ice water and chalky blue-strawberry, and Miles took the lid off, carefully spilling it all out near the curb.

"Hurry up, Miles," Leah said.

"I want to go home," Gabriela said, the first words she'd said all morning.

I could see Leah was worn out, and I wanted to go too, to get away from the courthouse as fast as I could, but nearby, also below the sidewalk, there was another paper cup. It was smaller, crushed. There was a ragged tear at the rim of the cup, and some red, tree floss that had blown inside, but it wasn't dirty.

Moon-white.

"Mad-die, can we please get out of here?" Leah stuck her head out the window and called out to me.

"Just give me another minute, Mom."

I didn't have my camera, but I could pick up the cast-off and use it in a collage later. I bent down to take it with me. It needed salvaging from the gutter.

CHAPTER 4

WHEN WE GOT HOME, GABRIELA HEADED straight upstairs to her bedroom. I followed my parents into the kitchen. Our ancient air conditioning was barely wheezing with warm air, but Leah and Miles didn't seem to pay much attention to the thermostat, celebrating the judge's ruling by cracking open some sparkling apple cider. Leah and Miles had gotten rid of all the alcohol in the house ever since Jordan had his "problems," they called it, their way of glossing over Jordan's jail times to their friends.

Miles offered me a glass. "No thanks," I said.

"It's all good, all good." Miles said, raising his glass in the air.

"But Jordan's not out of the woods yet," I said, watching them clink their glasses. "Another violation and he'll be sent up to Chino. That's not just jail. It's a hardcore state prison."

"We have to be optimistic," Leah said, and Miles put his arm around her shoulder. Leah took a quick sip, then put down her glass and looked at her watch. "I'm late," she said. Her regular art classes at Taft High School didn't start until late August, but she was teaching a summer art class at Valley College. "Can you please make sure Gabby eats something before she gets picked up for her soccer game," she said as she was rushing out the door. "She didn't eat a thing before we left this morning."

"Sure, sure."

"I've got to get to the store too," Miles said, and left just after Leah. Twenty minutes later I was still sitting in the kitchen when Gabriela came down the stairs with a bulky soccer bag in one hand, a backpack slung over one shoulder, and iPod ear buds in her ears that drizzled white wires down the sides of her face.

"*Hola, mi amor,*" she said, as she let go of her soccer bag and dropped it on the kitchen floor.

"You've been watching too many *telenovelas*, Gabby."

"It wouldn't kill you to learn a little Spanish," she said as she untangled herself from the backpack. Then she flopped into a chair.

"I know enough."

Gabriela tapped her cleats on the floor. "I miss him you know, Maddie. I miss Jorge."

"It's Jordan I miss, the Jordan we used to know."

"Can't you give him a break, for once?" Gabriela pushed away the sandwich Leah had left for her on the table. "Why do you care so much that he changed his name?"

I nudged the plate back in her direction. "I care. Come on, Gabby. Eat something, will you?"

"I'm not hungry." She stood up. "Anyway, I have to get to practice. Bye."

She left and I looked down at the sandwich untouched on the plate, and I wrapped it up in aluminum foil for her, put it in the fridge, and headed off to work.

December 14, 2007

Dear Alex—

I land in Auckland, New Zealand, barely forty-eight hours before we're scheduled to depart. Auckland is in the heart of Polynesia, surrounded by volcanoes and black-sand beaches, rain forests and the red-flowered Pohutukawa trees, but I have no time explore or to be a tourist. The Esperanza has been docked for a couple of weeks on the Princess Wharf, loading up on provisions and refueling, and I report to the ship as soon as I arrive. I'm assigned a berth and settle in. It seems right that we depart from New Zealand, where stories of whale riders and the whales that guided the canoes of ancient Maoris are carved into wood and greenstone. I hope this mission to save whales will carve a new story.

We leave Auckland a couple of days later and head out to the Southern Ocean. There's a small crowd of people waving and cheering from the dock, but there's no one waving good-bye to me. I didn't tell anyone, except Jack, where I am or what I'm doing. I couldn't. You know our mom. Worries are like her oxygen, more so now, and Dad can't keep a secret, even when he tells me I should keep mine locked away. So I'm here, completely alone, but for a moment I think I see you in the crowd on the dock. You're cracking that yeah-right, half-wink, funny smile of yours, and for that brief moment, I don't feel alone anymore.

People say that the Southern Ocean, encircling

Antarctica, is the most hostile of all oceans. Sea
temperatures can vary from about 28 to 50 degrees
Fahrenheit with cyclonic storms that travel eastward
around the continent and frequently intensify because of
the temperature contrast between the ice and the ocean.

The Esperanza is seventy-two meters long, with a top
speed of fourteen knots. Built in Poland, she was originally
ordered built by the Russian government in the 1980s to
serve as a fire-fighting vessel, but the ship has an ice-class
status and can navigate through the Polar Regions. It has
five decks and a helicopter landing pad.

From the minute I step onboard, I know that nothing
in my life has prepared me for this—not my half-assed
attempt at film school; not the training or briefings from
experts; not the Esperanza's webcam, which I watched for
hours; not the many days you and I spent together on
Jack's sailboat to Baja; not even the onboard training I did
on the North Sea. And I know doubt has already crept into
every muscle of my body. I can feel it in every soft tissue
and molecule.

Standing on the bridge, I can almost feel the bones of
the ship too, all metal, under me and over me, swallowing
me up. Crazy, it feels good, but I can smell a hundred
storms ahead.

Everything I thought I knew is different here, on our
way to the Southern Ocean. There's all light and no
darkness in the summer season, which is November to
March in the Southern Hemisphere. The proximity to the
pole scrambles your perception, and it's disorienting not
knowing the time of day. Night isn't really night as we
know it, just a sky bathed in purple-blue. The sun seems to

follow an opposite track, and the phases of the moon appear to run in reverse order. The constellations are inverted, and I wonder what you would say about that, because you were always saying stuff like, "Things were written in the stars." But maybe you were right.

So, here I am, where there's almost twenty-four hours of light, the winds blowing like crazy, NNW, upturned stars, and I'm hanging upside down in a ship at the bottom of the earth.

Al—ways—
Aiden

CHAPTER 5

MY AFTERNOON SHIFT AT THE SUPERMARKET started with three twenty-minute brownouts and continued with the lights flickering on and off all day long and registers rebooting again and again. I'd only worked a half-shift, but by the time I finished work, I was glad to put my checker apron away and get out of there.

I tried texting Bryn again.

Miss u.

I saw the text delivered and read, but there was nothing back from her.

That would be the last time I text her, I swore to myself.

Outside, I was about to go to my car and meet Aiden at the park, but near the front entrance I saw a few people milling around a fold-up table stacked with handouts and I stopped to look. Behind the table there was a big sign with the usual earthquake tips I'd heard and read before—duck under a desk or sturdy table, stay away from windows, bookcases, and file cabinets. Watch out for falling plaster and ceiling tiles. Hold onto your cover. If it moves, move with it. But there was something else in bold, fire-jacket-yellow letters.

You Can Save a Life.
Join CERT: Your Community Emergency Response Team
New classes start July 15.

On another part of the sign there were photos—one photo of a building on fire, another of the top of a car inundated in water, and a third crackling with lightening across a dark sky.

I picked up one of the flyers and skimmed over the program. There was training for fire safety and fire suppression techniques, earthquake awareness, search and rescue, and first aid. On the back of the flyer was a schedule for classes and training that was beginning a week from today and would be held at multiple locations, the community college, a local fire station, and one of the parks.

You Can Save a Life.

I picked up a pen and wrote my name, email, and phone number on the clipboard, and was about to leave when I turned around and came back to the table.

Add one more.

This could be good. This could be the answer for him.

And I add another name just below mine, Jordan's.

CHAPTER 6

I T WAS LATE AFTERNOON WHEN I ARRIVED AT THE
state park where Aiden had said he'd be. The small
park was tucked away and barely visible from the main
street. The plaque out front said it had once been one of
the rest stops on the old El Camino Real mission trail.
There was a long, nine-room Spanish adobe built in the
mid-1800s, a two-story French-style limestone house,
and a small pond. I'd been to this park before, but there
was something very different on the grounds today, a
freestanding rock wall in one of the open, grassy areas.

I picked out Aiden easily from afar. He was wearing
jeans, but his shirt was crisp—white and neat. He was
playing blitz chess with an older man, and both were
hunched over a chessboard on a picnic table in the shade
of a grove of crooked trees, each one making a move
then landing a palm on the knob on the timer.

He saw me and waved. "There she is, my good luck
charm," Aiden called out, getting up from the picnic table
and walking over to give me a hug. It was a quick embrace, but it felt good and I reached around him, below

his arms to his waist, and hugged him back. "I've been waiting for you," he said. "Here, sit down," and he tapped the empty space on the bench near him. "This guy here has been beating me, and bad," he laughed, introducing me to Jack, his dad's Navy buddy with whom he was staying. Jack's face was sun creased, much like the wet tea-bag staining a paper napkin near the chessboard, but his eyes were sharp. He lived near the park, and he'd been a key grip for Paramount, Aiden said, rigging cameras and mounting them on dollies, jibs, and cranes. He used to let Aiden hang out with him on movie sets when Aiden was a kid.

Aiden wasn't holding his book this time, but it was there, propped up on a pile of papers near his feet. It looked beat-up and yellowing, the kind of paperback Gabriela would buy for fifty cents at a neighborhood garage sale.

"Feeling better today, I hope?" Aiden asked me.

I felt grounded by the knobby trees that spilled out their roots above ground, and whatever it was that had made me lightheaded and unsteady the other day was gone. "Much better." I looked over to the rock wall. "I've never seen one of those here in this park."

"Oh that? I helped set it up, and I'll be supervising some climbing demos tomorrow," Aiden said, knocking down one of Jack's knights. "It's part of a presentation I do once in a while, for Greenpeace."

"Greenpeace?" I'd heard about the environmental

group, but it was the way his voice trailed off when he said the name that made me take out my camera. I put it low to the ground, casually, as though I was just setting it down, but I pointed the lens in Aiden's direction. It hardly made a sound when I took the photo, just a tiny whoosh. The sun was very bright, and I had to cup my hand over the screen so that I could review the photo and I realized I'd miscalculated the light. My stealth photo of Aiden's backlit face looked a little grainy, and by mistake I'd also captured the edge of Aiden's book.

"Checkmate," Aiden called out, minutes later, with a final smack of the timer.

"You got me," Jack said. "But how about this? Bet you can't name the best chess scene in a movie," Jack challenged Aiden.

Aiden thought for a moment. "James Bond, *From Russia With Love*, 1963?"

"Hmmm. Close. But I think it's gotta be *Casablanca*, 1942? " Jack lobbed back, laughing. "Bogie in a white tuxedo, his cigarette smoke in the air. Now that's a scene."

"I have to check out the rock wall before tomorrow. But I need a belayer. Would you?" He turned to ask me.

"Belayer?"

"It's the person who stands below and holds onto the rope so the climber won't fall. Don't worry. I can teach you."

I was curious and followed him to the freestanding wall, which was pockmarked with dozens of multi-colored climbing holds and grips, and surrounded with a thick padding. The grips reminded me of the pots of colors in a watercolor pan set, but I still had no idea what belaying really entailed. Before I knew it, he'd put on a harness then showed me how to get into mine. He pulled a rope through some kind of buckle, connected something else he called a karabiner and attached it to my harness, and as he did, his hand lingered just lightly on my hips.

He handed me some gloves. "You're the one who controls the rope and the speed."

I looked up to the top of the sheer twenty-foot wall. "And you trust me to do this?"

"I do. The key is never to let go of the rope," he laughed.

I held the rope and listened to his instructions carefully. I had to make sure there was friction and that he had the right amount of rope by paying out or pulling in excess rope, he said. To prevent a fall, I had to hold the rope in a lock position on what he called the "dead" rope with both hands, on one side of my body, one at my waist, the other, at my hip. Then he did some safety checks and went over the instructions and commands again.

"Ready?"

I wasn't, but I nodded yes, and he began. I watched him grab onto the first grip. "It's like a puzzle," he said, looking up. He rotated his hips toward the wall, finding his center of gravity, and stepped up the wall, using his toes rather than the balls of his feet.

He stepped up to the next grip. "Give me a little

slack," he said, and I fed what he'd described to me as "live" rope carefully upward toward him. But I had to watch him and try to anticipate his next move, letting out slack and still always keeping at least one hand on the brake side of the rope.

I started to sweat.

"More slack," he called out again, this time about halfway up the wall, but then he called out "up rope," and I struggled to take in the slack. "You're doing great," he called down to me. "More tension," he said, almost at the top. I took a long breath when he reached the summit.

"How about staying up there for a while," I joked, but my hands were shaking.

"No chance of that," he called down to me.

Coming down was the hardest part, I knew, and it was up to me to control his rate of descent. He'd warned me about the reflex to grab onto an out-of-control live rope, and I kept repeating that warning to myself.

"Lower," he called out.

"Lowering," I said, and he swung down slowly.

Everything was going well until he got three-quarters of the way down the wall. The rope seemed to snag, then run away from me and I panicked. I don't know what happened, but I did exactly what I wasn't supposed to do and grabbed on to the live rope as it ran away from me, down the length of my gloves. Aiden fell first, but compressed himself into a ball, then rolled back.

Then I fell backwards, with a splat, but the padding below us seemed to absorb both our falls.

"Sorry," I called, still on my back and breathing hard, and I could feel the adrenaline continue to pump in my temples.

"Hey, you did great, considering it was your first time," he smiled, and helped me up from the mats. He unhooked my harness for me, and his hands again felt good at my waist. "Next time you'll be the climber, and I'll teach you how to fall, how to dissipate the energy of the fall." I took off my gloves and he looked at my palms. "Lucky you, even with gloves you can sometimes get a rope burn," he said, then poured half a bottle of cold water over both my palms. "Could have been worse. Here, drink the rest of this," he said, handing me the water bottle.

I drank it down in one long gulp.

"So what about you?" he asked. "You haven't told me what you do," he said, watching me intently for my answer.

"I'm supposed to go to art school in New York, but now I'm not so sure. I make these mixed media collages. I submitted a portfolio of a series of surreal landscapes, combining different skylines, urban with desert and night with day, and I guess the admissions people must have thought they were okay."

"But you don't think so?"

"I don't know anymore."

"Why?"

I told Aiden about my dry spell. "More like a scorched earth spell," I joked, and Aiden leaned over and gave me a hug.

"You'll have to show them to me, your collages. But everyone goes through a creative slump. You'll be okay. You will," he said, but it was as though he wasn't only trying to reassure me, but himself too. It was a long and drawn-out embrace, and I took in the smell of him, all of him, the soapy scent of his shirt and the warmth of his skin.

Later, we rejoined Jack and walked with him to the man-made lake, which was completely surrounded by fencing. Jack flung some bird feed out over the fence, and talked about how he used to assemble the camera equipment according to the director of photography's specifications, describing how he would push, mount, or hang the camera equipment from a variety of settings including hundred-foot cranes and helicopters.

"I had to do a lot of measuring and calculating in those days. Boring memories, eh?" Jack stopped and reflected, chuckling.

"No. No. I want to hear more. And any photo tech advice you can give me." I liked Jack and his anecdotes about his movie crews.

"Looks like your good luck charm worked," Jack said to Aiden, just after a park ranger let us know that the park was closing, and Aiden started to pack up the chess gear.

Aiden put his arm around me. "Sure did. I'll pack up the rest of our stuff and meet you at the car."

Jack turned to me when Aiden left to go to the car and was out of earshot. "There's a trick to overcoming backlight. A little flash fill will make up for it. But of course, that's only if you don't mind that your subject is aware of the fact that you're taking a photo of him."

"You saw me?" I flushed a little.

"Yeah, sorry. I got a glimpse of your screen, and I wanted to tell you that backlight can sometimes be truer to life. The photo might not be perfect, but it can bring out a person's real state of being, and I think you got Aiden just right, with the book and all–" Jack stopped.

"What do you mean?"

Jack turned to me. "He told you about the book, right?"

"The book? No. Actually not."

Jack coughed and looked like someone who'd said too much, quickly changing the subject. "You know, you can't always hide behind a camera. Sometimes you have to go all in, right up in a person's face. It's not about apertures or F-stops or megapixels."

By this time we'd reached the pond floodgate, which was in the shape of a giant iron horseshoe. Only a few metal bolts fixed the iron to the stone that lined the pond and held up the floodgate. The stone and metal seemed so securely fastened together, safe from flooding, despite its age.

Jack told me about how the pond was fed by an ancient artesian well, and used to drain into a stream that fed into the Los Angeles River, but now emptied into the concrete flood-control system.

The sun was starting to set. "It was the Chumash Indians who came before the Spaniards. There was a village here, centuries before. There's only one photograph, from the 1930s, a WPA, public works project photo that shows a lone tree on an Indian burial mound that hints of their existence," Jack said.

"What happened to the mound?" I asked.

"It was bulldozed back in the '40s to make room for suburbia. But sometimes you can feel them, you know?" Jack said, looking back at the park.

"Who?"

"The spirits of the Chumash. They believed that a part of a person's spirit always stays in the earth where the body was buried, and that the remains should never be separated from the spirit."

When we reached Aiden's car, he was leaning against the window and looking up, the last rays of the sun washing over his face. He smiled at us, and I felt them too, the spirits.

January 1, 2007

Dear Alex—

Every person onboard has a job to do. The professional crew includes the captain, a radio operator, a logistics coordinator, chief engineer, cook, and a boatswain. Most are old sea dogs from way back. The rest of us are newbie volunteer deck hands. The ship has over thirty berths, and I share a cabin with three other volunteers. Our cabin is located at the front of the ship, and when the sea gets rough the porthole becomes completely submerged and looks like a washing machine on a crazy wash cycle.

We get a wake-up call around 7:00 a.m., then breakfast at 8:00 in the mess. The tables look like picnic tables you'd find in a park, except the seats have better cushioning.

Our cook says he has the toughest job, preparing food for so many different kinds of palates. We have an international crew, over thirty people from sixteen countries, some Brits, others Dutch, Japanese, Aussies, and a few Spanish-speaking. Dad used to say that mess decks are the heart of any ship, and now I know he's right.

After we eat we get to our assigned chores. This week I'm on mess duty, wiping down the galley counters and cleaning the floors. I seem to be good at mess duty when I'm not trying to film, and when I'm not sick as a dog. There's something strangely comforting about the loose tendrils of the mop and the motion of twisting the water out in the bucket. Somehow, the mop is the one thing that doesn't slip out of my hands, and it's a good thing too because losing a mop or a bucket overboard is considered bad luck on a ship. My crazy Aussie cabin mate warned me about that, then he printed out a list for me of all the things that can bring bad luck on a ship, including whistling, throwing stones into the sea, and opening a tin can from the bottom. I kidded him about it, mercilessly, but after just a few days on the island of a ship that's on the sea, I find myself latching on to any superstition, any myth.

There are other jobs, like chipping rust off the metal deck, coiling ropes to keep the decks clear, painting, standing watch, but that's for later, when my sea legs finally kick in.

I'm one of a few new volunteers, and many of us have gotten some of our activist stripes on land, campaigning against pollution and toxins, deforestation, oil drilling, and genetically engineered ingredients. But even those who were on the North Sea training are still untested, especially me.

Evenings, some of the crew play chess and backgammon. Sugar packet football is big here. The rules are simple to learn. We each take a turn sliding the packet across, and see who gets it closest to the edge of the table without the packet falling off. The tournaments can go on for hours.

The games are good. They open people up. The old guys, "salts" they call them, love to tell us newbies their war stories. An ocean campaigner veteran tells the story about the time the endangered blue fin tuna were freed from their cages by a flotilla of inflatable boats in the Mediterranean off Malta. The flotilla surrounded the circle of netting, he tells us, poking holes to release the endangered species. It's a short road from endangered to extinction, the ocean campaigner tells us.

I go back to my bunk, but I can't sleep. The word "extinction" keeps floating around in my head. The thought of erasure, as if something had never existed, doesn't leave me. What if I forget you? What if you go extinct in my memory? My memories of you and your existence are my endangered species, and I can't let that happen.

A couple of days later, we ring in the New Year; 2008. There's a party in the mess hall and a little too much wine. We count down to midnight, but numbers and dates and months and years seem out of place here. The New Year doesn't stop me from asking myself the same question. Can I do this for you?

Al—ways—
Aiden

CHAPTER 7

AIDEN JUMPED INTO THE PASSENGER SEAT OF MY car, his book in hand. I looked at him and it seemed impossible that I'd only known him for one week.

"Thanks for giving me a ride. This is the second time this month my car is in the shop."

"No worries," I said. Where do you need to go?"

"Just get on the 405 heading south," he said, and his hand found a resting spot near my knee.

While I was driving, I told him about the CERT classes I'd signed up for. Somehow, I wanted him to be the very first to know.

He gave me a thumbs up. "So, what is it that you're reading all the time?" I asked.

"I've been wondering when you were going to get around to asking me," he said, giving me a crinkly-eyed smile. He flipped the book over for me to see.

"*Moby Dick*? Really?" I vaguely remembered trying to tackle the novel in ninth grade, its archaic, nineteenth-century language, and the long, run-on sentences. Every chapter was full of random, oddball characters with strange names. One thing I did remember clearly though—the fact that I never did get through more than a quarter of the way through the book.

"The name Starbuck appears 196 times in *Moby Dick*," Aiden said. "He was the first mate of the ship, the *Pequod*, you know. He was the only one who challenged Captain Ahab about killing the whale."

"One hundred and ninety six times?" The three-digit number sidetracked me from his description of the character. Was Aiden a numbers person too? A minute ticked by. Close to him, I noticed a little stubble on his face, and just a tinge of darkness under his eyes. I waited another moment but he failed to continue his explanation and I couldn't think of anything more to say.

"Sorry, I get distracted easily," he apologized. "But I told you that, right off the bat, remember?" he said.

"Right."

Traffic was light and twenty-five minutes later we arrived at the post-production studio where Aiden worked. The building was huge, a warehouse-like structure that took up almost half a block, the parking lot almost empty.

"Want to come in?" Aiden asked.

"You sure it's okay?"

"It's usually just me and maybe one other guy here on the night shift," Aiden said. "And the cleaning crew," he added, smiling.

"All right," I said, and parked the car.

Inside, there was a high ceiling, industrial lighting, and exposed air ducts. A string of offices lined the edges, the middle filled up with a maze of small cubicles. "Welcome to 'the pit.'"

He showed me to his cubicle, which had a desk and a couple of small screens. Many of the newer reality TV shows had a high shooting ratio, he said, and before editing the footage, someone had to log in the source material, labeling the content and clips for editing.

Aiden sat down at the desk in his cubicle. "But I've also been doing some extra editing on the side too, and I think my supervisor is going to give me a promotion. But for now, it gets kind of boring here at night, just logging in hours and hours of raw footage. Everyone calls it the dark closet of production," he laughed. "So sometimes I bring in other stuff to watch, classics. Last night, I brought in a DVD of *The Misfits,* directed by John Huston. He directed *Moby Dick* too."

"So we're back to *Moby Dick?*" I laughed.

"John Huston was one of the all-time great directors," Aiden said, "a real rebel," and for a moment Aiden was a thousand miles away. "He said that directing a picture meant coming out of your own loneliness and making a small world, then putting a frame around it."

I moved the mouse on the desk and the screen lit up with a scene paused on the black and white image of a horse, blurred in motion. "I get that part . . . about putting a frame around a small world."

I sat down next to Aiden and touched the screen. "What's this? Can I see it?"

"I don't know. It's probably the toughest scene in the movie, Maddie," he cautioned, and he sounded like Miles when he was being protective. "Those beautiful, wild horses," he suddenly said. "Captured . . . for what? For the slaughterhouse? For dog food?"

It was the seminal scene of the movie, he said, filmed in the early 1960s in a dry lakebed in the Nevada desert. "Some loser horse wrangler pilots a prop plane low to the ground to run down wild horses from the mountains into an open area. Then two cowboys follow the terrified horses in a speeding pickup truck, catching and roping them up. It's not a pretty sight."

"I want to see it too."

He pressed play, and I saw a flat horizon.

The clouds are rainless, and there is only the heat and gray shimmer of the desert.

In black and white, the scene was jarring. The horses' manes flew upwards, their legs kicking against the chafing lassos tied to old truck tires. One horse stood up on its hind legs, fighting against the ropes, but the truck and the lassos wouldn't stop until they were all beaten down to the ground, their legs tied up like rodeo cattle.

I wanted to turn away from it, but I couldn't move. I looked at Aiden and he looked beaten down, too. He hit the pause button, and I reached out to take his hand. His hand relaxed in mine, but he was quiet, and I could see he was still reliving the scene. Then he closed his eyes and took a long breath.

"It doesn't end like that, does it?" I asked, and my hand trembled as I pressed down on the play button.

The scene continued, dust and sweat mixed in the air, along with the cries of the horses until finally one of the cowboys, dirty and worn down, drove the pick-up truck from horse to horse. I could hear the sound of the truck engine, coarse and raspy as it raced across the desert flats. I held my breath as the cowboy slashed the ropes with a knife, and freed the horses.

The horses ran off into the desert, and we fell into each other's arms. Aiden held me close, but then I could feel him holding back, and his body retreated from me.

CHAPTER 8

TWO DAYS LATER, MY MANAGER LET ME OFF WORK a half hour before my shift ended, and I decided to make a quick pit stop at home to change clothes before seeing Aiden. At home, Leah's hodgepodge of ceramic pots on the doorstep looked neglected and unwatered, stems wilting, and the doormat had faded to a purplish black and blue. I made a mental note to tell my mom that she was taking the new water restrictions a little too seriously.

The front door was ajar, and I walked through the small entry room and then down a narrow hallway. Twenty-one photos of Jordan, Gabriela, and me lined the walls, exactly seven of each, but they were all just a bit off, as though someone had walked by in a hurry and knocked them a few degrees crooked. Even before I heard the voices, I knew something was wrong.

"I promise you, I'm not using. I swear it. They'd let me go home if you said it was okay with you, Mom," I heard Jordan say.

Leah and Jordan were standing in the living room arguing, but Leah was near the fireplace, and Jordan way

60

off on the other side of the room near the large bay window. Leah was wearing her newest yoga outfit, soft, loose pants and a no-iron top, but she looked rumpled today. Her hands gripped the fireplace as though she were hanging onto a lifeboat. In the background I could hear the TV on in the den. Neither Leah nor Jordan heard me come in and I could have slipped away, but I was glued to my spot in the hallway.

"I need proof," Leah pressed her lips together hard, and her hands fluttered to her sides. She looked tired and small against the old fireplace, swallowed up by the cold brick hearth.

"Proof? You're sounding just like Dad. But if that's what you want, I'll take a drug test every day, I promise. I promise you!"

"I want to believe you, but I don't know if I can," Leah said, not moving away from the fireplace. "Did you get a job?" she asked, looking at him hopefully.

"Not exactly."

I moved just a bit closer and leaned against the hallway wall. From my new vantage point I could see better. Leah and Jordan continued to argue, the back and forth between them the same old script—Jordan sounding like he'd finally gotten his act together, and Leah both hopeful and suspicious at the same time. There were things Jordan had done that my parents didn't even know about, but I knew—the phones and cameras he'd shoplifted and sold, the times I'd seen him dealing drugs in the park, the cars he'd keyed in the school parking lot, and the debit card he'd swiped from Miles's wallet.

"I really want to come home, Mom. That new rehab place the court sent me to is bullshit."

Sick to my stomach, I stormed into the living room. "'I really want to come home? The rehab is bullshit?'" I mimicked Jordan. "Just stop it, Jordan."

"It's *Jorge*," Jordan reminded me, his eyes glassy. "And is that all you got?"

"Don't you get it? This probation is your last chance." Then I caught a glimpse of the black, electronic monitor Jordan now wore on his ankle.

"You like my little ankle biter?" he asked, smiling and lifting up the bottom of his pants. "What are you doing here, anyway, Maddie?" he scoffed. "Aren't you busy being the good little girl, who finished high school early and has a job, and who's going off to New York City?"

"It's all right, Maddie," Leah said, one hand still holding onto the mantel. The thick wood ran across the length of the fireplace and displayed every Little League trophy Jordan had won in elementary school

I took a long breath. "I just signed up for CERT. You know, the Community Emergency Response Team training," I said to Jordan. "We could do it together, you and me, like we used to do?"

But Jordan ignored me and hung his head, morphing into his version of contrite son. I knew what was coming next. Worse than Jordan's long list of screw-ups was how he always tried, and very often succeeded, in making everyone feel sorry for him.

"It's my birthday soon," he said, right on cue, turning to Leah, and still ignoring me. He said it in his best sweet-talking voice, the honey-tongued tone he used to pick up girls.

Leah sighed softly. "Jordan," she said, as though he was still little Jordan, and I could tell that Jordan thought he had Leah right where he wanted her.

"Hey, Maddie," Jordan said. "You don't want me to miss my birthday, do you?" he asked, his eyes suddenly softening. "C'mon. Can you help me out here, Mads?"

I saw it too, just a quick flash in his expression, that part of him that was still ten-year-old Jordan, smiling in his red fireman's hat on his birthday, the matching napkins and plates Leah had bought especially for the party, the paper cups that looked like miniature fire hydrants. But he wasn't that sweet Jordan anymore. He was the guy who shaved his head, joined the North Hollywood Boys gang, and renamed himself Jorge.

My face went fire hot. "Help? But that's what I'm trying to do. What about that training I started to tell you about? Don't you think it would be—?"

Jordan rolled his eyes at me. "I heard you. But some lame emergency training? Really?"

"But you haven't heard me out. I—"

Jordan interrupted. "That's your big idea for me? You and your *suggestions*," he said.

"But—"

Jordan turned away from me and walked out.

Ten seconds later, the front door slammed.

"Maddie? What's he talking about? What suggestion?" Leah took a breath, finally letting go of the fireplace, and walked toward me, her arms outstretched.

"It's nothing. You know Jordan. He'll cool down. I'm sorry, I really have to go too," I said, and gave Leah a hug.

"What did he mea—?" Leah didn't finish her question. She turned off the TV and cocked her head to one side, and I knew she was listening, hoping for the sound of Jordan returning through the front door.

"I just came home to get something."

"Okay." Leah's arms crumpled and she walked me to the door through the narrow hallway. As she did, she stopped for a moment at every crooked photograph, looking at each one for a moment, and then straightened them out, one by one.

January 3, 2008

Dear Alex—

*There's a woman onboard from Canada. Her name's
Olivia. She's a climate campaigner and our ship scientist.
She's tiny, but no beginner at non-violent direct actions,
and she has the most earnest look on her face, even though
she's a little older than most of the volunteers. She was one
of the coordinators of the action to sink large-scale models
of Big Ben and the Pyramids in the Caribbean, trying to
show the dangers of global warming and rising seas, but
she's also been on the harsher winter campaigns, when
there's complete darkness, and where the sea ice constantly
forms and moves. I think she's like one of those chameleons
we once saw with Mom and Dad at the San Diego Zoo.
She seems to fit in anywhere she's sent, shifting and
adapting herself to any kind of condition.*

*On this campaign, her deck assignment is painting,
and I watch her as she follows the curve of the railings,
dipping her brush into the paint can lightly, then frugally
spreading the pigment on the metal. She wears no jewelry
except for a leather bracelet on her wrist, no makeup, her
red hair tied up in an uneven braid beneath a wool cap.*

*After dinner, she takes out an old but beautiful deck
of Tarot cards. They're large and intricate, with gold leaf
on the rounded edges. We sit in the mess hall after dinner
and she entertains the crew with her outrageous
prophecies.*

*"I see it in my Tarot cards, when the winds blows
SSE," she always begins, as though she's telling a ghost*

story around a campfire and everyone starts hooting and
howling.

We laugh at her interpretations of The Devil, The
Star, and The Hermit, but there are little fragments of
truth in her comical forecasts from her twenty-two-card
deck. Tonight she predicts a plot, the open rebellion of one
of our crewmembers, and some of us almost believe she's
another mole, like the double agents who were planted on
our North Sea training ship to mess with our heads, but I
don't think so, and I know you'd like her Tarot cards and
her stories.

She knows every inch of the Esperanza, every dark
niche and cubby hole, every switch on the bridge and in the
engine room, the flat drawers in the chart room, and she
shows me where I can position my camera to get the best
shots. She takes me up to the Monkey Island, the ship's
top-most accessible height. There, she points out angles no
one else sees. She does this for me even though she's on to
me and knows I'm no better than a stowaway. She knows
I'm a pretender, that I talked my way on board for this
action like a glib salesman, giving everyone the impression
I was a seasoned filmmaker, padding my pitiful resume,
when I'm just a complete phony.

Olivia figured it out right off, but she keeps my secret
as if it were her own. She holds on to it without a wink or
even a conspirator's smile. She keeps and abets my secret
for me quietly, under the cold lid of her paint can. She
doesn't know yet, that I have another, a worse secret, for
which this trip is my penance and my promise.

Al—ways—
Aiden

CHAPTER 9

LOOKED AROUND THE PARKING LOT OF TWAIN'S, THE fifties-era diner where I was supposed to meet Aiden. I didn't see his car, but someone had parked a tricked-out gold Mustang convertible just outside the back door. The car's shiny rims kept spinning around, even after the engine was shut off, and my head started spinning a little too.

I went inside. The L-shaped diner was bustling with a noon lunch crowd and all the booths were occupied. The hostess apologized to me, and I propped myself against the wall near the entrance, waiting for Aiden and a table to free up. I looked around. The shop was decorated with what looked like the original plaid carpeting and tufted, fake-leather booths. There were low, swivel counter chairs and two stone walls, the tables in a faux-wood Formica, the holes in the booth seats taped up with silver duct tape.

Suddenly, a noisy AC vent sputtered above me, and Aiden blew in from the front entrance. "Don't you just love this greasy spoon throwback?" He smiled, looking up at the one wobbly ceiling fan. "Jack turned me on to this place. He and his crew used to come here after shoots at all hours of the night. Wait 'til you see the menus. They've got a sketch of Mark Twain."

Up close to him, I smelled a faint trace of saltwater coming from his neck, and I thought I was back in chem class, where two reactive elements were being combined and were about to create a mini explosion.

He looked at me and gave me a kiss on the forehead. Finally, a booth opened up and we sat together on one side and ordered some sandwiches.

"Look what I found under the table," he said. "A bunch of plastic compasses," and he looped his arm around my waist. "But it looks like they're all fixed at northeast."

"That's because they're not real, you know . . . not magnetized," I said, fighting a smile.

"I wonder if that means something, a sign of some sort."

"What kind of sign could that be?" but a creeping feeling came over me. Maybe the fixed compasses were a sign, and were pointing northeast for me, toward New York?

"Hey, look," he said. "I think one of them is actually moving."

"It's probably broken. It's just a toy, what's the difference?"

"Come outside with me. Let's check it out."

"Outside? It's boiling out there." More than the heat, I wished he would stay put so I could rest my eyes on him, drinking him in. But a moment later we were both at the back door.

There were dozens of empty cardboard boxes scattered around the parking lot behind the diner. Aiden walked up and down the length of the parking lot twice, holding up the compass in various positions.

"Well?" I was frying in the heat.

"You were right, they're not working. I'm an idiot looking for stupid signs. We should go back inside."

"Sure," I said, only half-guilty about being happy to return to the AC. But the minute we sat back down, a homeless person with a long beard and long, wild hair walked in from the street. He was talking to himself and waving his arms wildly, as though pushing phantoms away. Everyone in the diner stopped to stare as he grabbed a handful of napkins from the counter and started wiping down one table, then moved on to another and another.

"I'm the prophet," he mumbled, over and over again.

"Someone needs to get that bum out of here," a customer yelled to a waiter behind the counter, and a couple of tall guys stood up, looking as though they were ready to run the homeless man out.

"I'll just call the police," the waitress responded and was about to pick up the phone when Aiden suddenly called out to her.

"Hey, no need for that. Let me just talk to the guy," Aiden said. "I think I can get him to leave."

"Well, all right," the waitress conceded. "But if he doesn't go soon, I'm calling."

Aiden snatched a clump of napkins and began to

clean off the tables alongside the homeless man. As he was cleaning, Aiden talked quietly to the man, but I couldn't hear what he was saying to him. Aiden looked calm, as though he was talking down a suicide jumper perched on a ledge. But the man continued to mumble, ignoring Aiden.

I could feel the room tensing up. People were grumbling. I stood up and pulled out some more paper napkins, joining Aiden and the homeless man. I followed Aiden's lead, wiping the table in a circular motion, while Aiden continued to talk to the man. There was something soothing about the circular motion, I realized, almost like brushstrokes on a canvas. The homeless man suddenly looked up at me then Aiden, nodding to him, and then he left, leaving a trail of wadded up napkins behind him.

Everyone stood up and clapped, but Aiden shrugged it off and we went back to our table.

"The prophet. Wasn't there a character like that in your book?" I asked Aiden.

"You remember that?" Aiden asked, a faint smile lighting up his face, when his phone lit up with a message. He read it, scrolling carefully down then back up again to reread it. "I completely forgot, Maddie. Listen, I've got to get going."

"What? Now?"

"Sorry, I just have to go. I'm really late. I'll see you tomorrow?" he asked.

"Not sure."

"Come on." He looked at me. "*I will not go, said the stranger, till you say aye to me,*" he said.

"You're quoting, now?" I laughed.

"Say aye," he said, softly, with the same calming voice he'd used to win over the homeless man.

"Fine. Aye. Aye. Go. Go do what you have to do." I smiled at him.

He gave me a quick kiss and disappeared out the door just as I realized he'd left a small notebook on the table, and I ran out to the parking lot to give it to him.

The sunlight was blinding. I walked toward the main street, but didn't see him, then turned around in the opposite direction. Squinting, I cupped my hands over my eyes and finally spotted him, leaning against the hood of his car. He looked washed out, faded against the hot metal of the car.

I inched closer. He was talking on his phone, completely focused on his conversation. The heat was crushing and his face was red, but I could tell, it was more than the temperature. He paced back and forth away from his car. When he turned his back, I took a few more steps closer, edging to his car. At first, I didn't understand what I was seeing. It took me a minute to realize, and my mouth went dry.

It's a pastel of nursery room colors, the softest shade of pink. In the back seat, was a baby's car seat, empty of its passenger, but there it was. The soft indentation in the quilted cover was unmistakable, like a watermark on paper.

CHAPTER 10

A FEW DAYS LATER, TWENTY OF US FILED IN FOR our first day of training. We picked out our nametags from a box on the table at the front of the classroom. Everyone took a seat, and we were given a manual and bunch of handouts and forms to sign. I sat next to a girl named Angela who looked older than me, but reminded me a little of Bryn, and we decided we would buddy up and exchange notes if either one of us missed a session.

This was only Level 1, the initial seventeen-hour course. By Level 3, a team member would have to complete a total of eighty hours. But even on day one, there was already a lot of information to absorb. I'd taken a notebook along with me, and I scribbled notes about water storage, instructions on how to purify water with bleach, the best ways to secure furniture and strap down appliances, and the safe distance from live wires, but it was hard to keep up with everything they were throwing at us.

There were acronyms for everything and I wondered how I would remember them all.

LIES—Limit, Isolate, Eliminate, Separate

DEPT—Direct pressure, Elevate, Pressure Point, Tourniquet

RPM—Respiration, Perfusion, Mental Status

Jordan would have remembered it all. Even in middle school, he had perfect recall of even the smallest of details. I glanced over at the box on the table. There it was, the only one that was left.

Black lettering on white.

Hello, my name is—Jordan.

Subtract Jordan. His nametag is still unclaimed in the box.

CHAPTER 11

I WAS SLEEPING AND SWEATING. IT WAS THE SAME nightmare I'd had before, Jordan in a prison-orange jumpsuit, his hands and feet tied together with plastic cuffs. Then, near a freeway, I saw boys hanging upside-down by their belts, dangling and spray-painting their monikers on freeway signs over the river of traffic, helicopter spotlights aimed on their bodies. The helicopters were deafening as they circled round, again and again. Suddenly I was with the boys, upside-down too, and I fell with them into the stream of speeding cars below. Then I was lying prone on the asphalt, and I saw the cars, now scattered, crushed against each other. There was no sound, not even the sound of my own breathing, but this time I heard a baby's cry pierce the air.

I woke up, my heart thumping. Someone knocked on my bedroom door.

I looked at my alarm clock—6:07 a.m. It could only be one person that early in the morning.

Miles opened the door up a crack. "Maddie? You up?"

"I am now." I dabbed my forehead and neck with the

edge of the sheet, and he came in and sat on my bed. A bright, hot light was already streaming mercilessly into the room. "Isn't it too early to go to the money-pit? Even for you?"

It had seemed like a good idea at the time, a well-known national mailbox store franchise, and Miles had landed a great rental in a prime location in Beverly Hills, but the store never really made much money. I knew Miles liked the orderliness of the post boxes, neatly lined up from floor to ceiling. But I also knew that the hose spewing Styrofoam peanuts could never fill up Miles's empty spaces, all those pages of calculations about wing-spans and velocity that he would never make again.

"I don't know. Couldn't sleep."

"So?" I could tell he was trying to tell me something. For years, he'd been sure that his ex-Boeing brat, his little math geek, would attend Cal Tech, or at the very least UC Santa Barbara's school of engineering, not some alternative art school that only offered some sort of certificate program.

"Nothing important, just checking up on my girl," he said with a half-laugh, and the sound of his steady voice cooled me down. "*Contents Under Pressure?*" he asked. He loved to morph the instructions on the packing labels into his own brand of family pep talks.

Still, Miles's packing labels did seem to have some purpose. They were little clues as to what was hidden inside the sealed boxes—*Fragile, Perishable, Special Order.*

"So, Dad, are you *Handling* me *With Care*? Are you hoping I've come to my senses and decided against New York?"

"Very funny. Just haven't seen you around lately. What have you been doing with yourself?"

"Nothing much." I bit my lip.

"Anything else going on?" he asked, the edge of his mouth curling up into a smile.

My parents had probably gotten wind of Aiden, and I'd already planned on telling them about him, but not at 6:00 a.m. "Not really." Suddenly, the room felt stifling again and I needed air. I got up and opened all my bedroom windows.

"Well, if you've brought up New York, you know this is your future we're talking about. I don't want you to waste your talents."

"I know that." I swallowed hard. I had a hard time staying upset with him. His voice made me think of graph points that remained on the same plane, never climbing or descending. "Did you take your meds this morning?" I asked him. He was always forgetting his medication, not because he was absent minded, but because he was still in denial of the high blood pressure diagnosis three doctors had given him. Sometimes I'd count the pills left over in the prescription bottle just to make sure he'd taken them all.

"So you're checking up on *me* now?" This time it was deeper laugh. "I just want you to remember that it's your future."

"Da—ad," I groaned.

"Look, Maddie, what's important now is that this is a crossroads for you."

"Crossroads, right. But how's the store doing? Do you want me to come in and help organize or do the books for you?" Last time I was at the store I'd noticed the inventory was dwindling, along with accounts receivable.

"Changing the subject again, are we? Not to worry. I'm all caught up, everything's fine," he assured me. "I've got a handle on all the numbers."

"If you say so."

"Just wanted you to know we can talk, if you want," Miles said.

"Thanks," and my father got up, quietly closing my bedroom door behind him. I could hear him taking the stairs down to the kitchen then grabbing the sandwich Leah had prepared for him the night before. I knew, too, that he would take out the trash then take the back roads to the city, through the tunnel at the Sepulveda Pass. He would call the store's voicemail, like he always did, and forget that halfway through the tunnel, cut through solid rock, his cell phone would lose its signal.

CHAPTER 12

TRIED TO GO BACK TO SLEEP BUT MY PHONE RANG again.

"We have to talk, Maddie."

"Jordan?"

"Yes, it's me, *Jorge*. Please, Maddie. Can you meet me?"

An hour later I was on the main trail that followed a brush-lined path. It led to several smaller paths near the waters of the wildlife reserve. The trail was dusty, and there weren't very many people this early in the morning, only a lone birdwatcher with binoculars and a group of teenage boys huddled on the small bridge that crossed a shrunken creek. I walked quickly past them. Close by, model airplanes buzzed loudly, like swarms of bees in the sky. By the time I arrived my sandals, were covered with a thin layer of dirt. Jordan was sitting near the stone flood marker that looked like an ancient temple. Carved into the stone were markings indicating fifty-, hundred-, and thousand-year flood lines. But it had also been freshly spray-painted with red graffiti.

Jordan saw the look on my face and held up both hands, flipping them back and forth for me to see. "See, they're clean," he said. "I swear it wasn't me."

"I can see that."

"Thanks for coming, Maddie. I really appreciate it."

"Are you sure you're allowed to be here?" I asked.

Jordan lifted one pant leg. "My PO took it off yesterday. I'm a free agent now," he smiled. "I've been doing good."

A white egret flew overhead and landed in the water just beyond the marker. I guessed I still owed Jordan something for never coming on visiting days, not even once, not at Juvenile Hall in Sylmar or Camp Gonzalez, his probation boot camp. Gabriela would go, but I didn't want to see him in one of those places, locked up behind barbed wire fences.

I noticed a cut and a bruise above his left eye. "What's that?"

It's black and blue, like ink, blotted out.

"It's nothing, just a stupid beat down near the park."

"A beat down?" I touched the welt above his eyebrow and he flinched. "Are you okay? Did you report it to your PO?"

"It's nothing, and no use in doing that, Mads," he shrugged.

"Are you sure you're okay?"

"Just leave it alone, Maddie," he insisted.

"So what's this all about?"

"I wanted to tell you that I want to take some classes . . . but . . ."

"But what?"

"I could use . . . just a little money," he said, not meeting my eyes.

"Classes? What classes?"

"I don't want to say anything about it yet. But it's good, Maddie, and I promise you I'll pay you back."

"That's why you asked me to meet you here? To borrow money?" I shook my head. "Sorry."

"Come on. It'll only be for a little while, and it's not for *stuff* this time. I promise." I looked at him closely. He didn't look like he was using, but Jordan almost never did. He'd always been good at hiding his addictions. "I'm almost twelve months sober, going to AA and all. You can call my sponsor if you want."

I searched his eyes. "There's still room in the CERT class."

"You still don't get it, Maddie. I have to do this my own way, and in my own time."

I watched him bend down and pick up a seedpod from the path. "Here," he said, putting the pod in the palm of my hand. It was almost weightless, and I could barely feel it.

"That's the part that makes it airborne," he said, pointing to the delicate, wing-like covering.

"Stop it. I know what you're doing."

"Come on. You know you want it. You're just like Mom. You love stuff like this."

"I'm nothing like Leah. Remember? We have no genetic connection, no DNA."

"DNA isn't everything, Maddie." Then he paused for a moment. "And speaking of DNA, I was wondering why you've always been so dead set against contacting your birth parents."

"Because."

"Because what?"

"Because they gave me up for no good reason. It was just because of numbers."

"Numbers? I don't get it."

"They had three children before me. I was their fourth. One too many, I guess. They kept the other three."

"Are you sure of that?"

"That's what I know, and . . ."

Jordan's face suddenly went rigid. I looked to the far end of the short path and saw that the threesome I'd seen clustered on the bridge had appeared there. Two were holding spray paint cans, each one dripping with red paint. When they saw Jordan and me, one held up the spray can high above his head and shook it, then flashed Jordan a mad dog stare.

Jordan signaled for me to be quiet and planted his feet on the dusty ground. He moved only one step forward, but he was completely focused on the three at the end of the path.

The light bleaches their faces out.

I felt one of my knees starting to shake uncontrollably

and the nearby tree trunks seemed to lean sideways, pulling me away with them.

There were more stares aimed at Jordan, but he remained very still. The two with spray cans moved in closer. One started to spray a backwards "L" on a trail sign, when the other began arguing with him, their voices becoming louder and louder. I couldn't make out what they were saying, but Jordan could, and I could tell he knew he had the upper hand.

"Stupid wannabe taggers," Jordan said under his breath, his eyes still trained on them. It was the third one who backed away first. The other two continued to argue, then followed and disappeared from view.

Jordan relaxed his stance. He looked battered down, and reached out to touch my arm, but I stepped back. "I'm sorry about that," he said.

Jordan turned to look out at the water. A family of geese swam by, disappearing into the reeds. Jordan picked up a pebble from the path and threw it, the pebble skipping perfectly on the water. "Aren't you going to answer me, Mads?" he pressed me.

The white egret took off again then landed perfectly on a tiny island in the wetlands. The egret's wings flapped slowly, finding air, but I couldn't. The sun was beating down hard and I couldn't get a lungful. I dug out my wallet from my purse. Inside, folded up, was the unspent one-hundred-dollar bill Miles had given me for my last birthday and I unfolded it, and left it on top of the flood marker.

January 5, 2008

Dear Alex—

I've got my sea legs now, and I'm on the green bridge wing of the Esperanza whenever weather permits. Alex, you have no idea. Up on the highest part of the ship, there's only sea and sky. You are with me every minute here, and I'm beginning to embrace this complete sparseness, the absence of concrete and land, buildings and trees and all vegetation.

I stopped shaving. You'd have a good laugh at my bad beard. It doesn't grow in evenly. When I look at myself in the mirror, I hardly recognize the person I see. And that's good, because I didn't like the person I used to see before.

I've started doing the interviews with the professional crew and some of the new volunteers about our mission to stop the whale hunters. I brought very little equipment with me, and the lighting is lousy, but I'm trying to look like I know what I'm doing, as though I've done lots of documentary interviews before. But no one seems to care when I fumble. Everyone wants to tell their story and the reasons they've come on board, and I'm trying to listen more than worry about whether I'm getting it right.

The first interview is with the captain. His beard is clipped and neat, unlike mine, and he wears a baseball hat. He's commanded other ships, the Rainbow Warrior and the Arctic Sunrise, on other campaigns And even though he speaks quietly, his voice is firm.

Early one morning we come across our first pod of humpback whales, and the sight is impossible to put into words. Olivia leads the way to an inflatable, and we get in

then drift toward the pod with the engine off. I can see
their knobby heads swimming in groups of twos and threes,
some even groups of six. They are creatures beyond beauty,
cutting the surface of icy waters, each with two blowholes
sending mist up to the sky. They are blue-black, but their
undersides are a mottled white. Long folds under their
mouth look like pleats and I find myself breathing with
them, in their rhythm.

They leap and dive, breaching the water with grace.
Their large tail flukes, indented in the middle, pitch in and
out, lifting the surface of the water in their wake. Meters
long, they take a deep dive, arching their backs, slapping
the water and it's as if they're dancing together in a ballet
of spray and secrets underwater. And then I spot them, a
mother and her calf. The calf glides with its mother in
perfect sync, and the mother circles around us as if to show
off her offspring. She studies us with her orange-sized
brown eye, and kidney-shaped pupil. I put out my hand
and feel the smooth, rubbery slickness of her body.

Olivia puts a hydrophone under the water to
document the sounds of the whales. They seem so human.
It's only the males that sing, and they fill up our inflatable
with their otherworld mating sounds.

Olivia gives me a funny look and throws her head
back, laughing hard at me. It's a funny sound, her deep
sailor's laugh, coming from such a tiny body. She says she
loves to see the faces of the rookies on the ship at their first
encounter with a pod. She says it's the face of fathers
seeing their newborns for the first time.

Al - ways -
Aiden

CHAPTER 13

OUR SECOND TRAINING SESSION WAS OUT-doors in the park, a mock emergency drill. I was one of the victims. I was lying on the grass with thirty others sprawled near me, some splattered with fake blood, others already bandaged up. I was a head injury and was supposed to stay completely still and keep my eyes shut, but the sound of people moaning close by startled me, and my eyes blinked open for a moment.

"Close them," Angela ordered me.

I'd been on the other end of the exact same training exercise a couple of hours ago. I was the one who had made the triage assessments, deciding who needed immediate attention and who could wait. The assessments had to be made quickly and efficiently. We were taught to look for the rise and fall of the chest, the sounds of breathing, and how to apply direct pressure, elevate, or make a tourniquet. For shock, we were told to watch for pale, cool, moist skin, rapid shallow breathing, and disorientation. I learned how to make a leg splint from a cardboard box and immobilize the injury. But now, I was the one on the ground, and I felt a small rock at the bottom of my spine. I smelled the grass and dirt.

Orangey, the sun burns hot on my eyelids.

I closed my eyes tighter, but I couldn't block out the color. It swirled madly below my eyelids. Then I heard the sounds of someone being strapped to a board close by. I could hear the buckles being fastened, quickly.

That could be you, Jordan.

That could be you, on a gurney, shot and bleeding.

Someone else kneeled down and opened my mouth, checked my airway, then checked for shock and broken bones.

"Okay, everyone," the team leader yelled out. "We're good here for now."

I opened my eyes and rubbed them. First I saw green. It was the safety helmets, sea green above me. Then I saw the red tag, the tag for life-threatening injuries, they'd pinned to my sleeve.

CHAPTER 14

LATER THAT DAY, I PARKED IN FRONT OF MY UNCLE'S house up in the hills. The Buddha-head fountain at the entrance had been turned off, but a trickle of water still ran down its half-closed eyes. Everything yielded to gravity in the hills. It seemed to pull down everything, even the thinnest stream of water that appeared when people watered their lawns or emptied out their pool. Only the ivy defied gravity, climbing up old oaks and pines, creating little wild patches of shadowy forest. I was happy I was early and would have the house to my-self for a bit before Aiden arrived.

I unlocked the front door and turned off the alarm.

Uncle Phil and Adele, both psychologists, were away for a couple of weeks, and Phil had left me the keys so I could water the indoor plants and also enjoy the pool. Unlike our chaotic household, their architectural, mid-century house was minimal, furnished with sleek sofas and a concrete dining room table, and entirely serene, as though the house itself was on Zoloft. It had an open palette of glass, concrete and steel, balanced on one side with an overhang which shaded the driveway, while another over the side patio allowed sun to stream through.

A clean and empty palette for Aiden to open up to me.

Through the living-room window I could see the day was going to remain hazy. I caught a glimpse of one of Leah's beautiful outdoor sculptures. Constructed from honeycomb aluminum, it picked up even the haziest of light. It was one of the few sculptures Leah had actually installed; the rest remained long-neglected and relegated to the back of our garage.

Waiting for Aiden, I wandered into the guesthouse near the pool. In the bathroom was a wall of bamboo cabinets filled with white towels and lotions, scented soaps and sprays. I was following the woven tatami mats that led to a stone and glass shower when I heard the doorbell ring.

I ran back to the front of the house and opened the door for Aiden.

He had the biggest smile on his face. "You are so beautiful, Maddie."

Beautiful. The word was so unexpected, I had to make an effort not to roll my eyes, but I couldn't help it. No one had ever said that to me before, no one except Leah, every night when she used to brush out my hair.

"You don't believe it?"

"Not really."

"That makes you even more so," he added with a laugh.

Outside, the rectangular pool area was flanked on one side by a row of teak chaises and striped cushions, almost like a hotel, the pool itself the latest in Pebble-Tech, a greenish-blue. Aiden chose a chaise and I dragged a chair over to sit nearby.

"Nice place to take a dip in this heat. You come here a lot?"

I could hear the automatic pool pump turning on, waking up the robo pool skimmer that looked like a whacked-out hose weaving around the pool. "Some-times." I knew how to swim, but even though we'd been to Phil's house several times over the summer, today was the first time I'd gone anywhere near Phil's long, saltwater pool. "But I don't like that thing," I said, pointing to the skimmer.

"I can fix that," he said, and he went over to the pool equipment on the side of the house and turned off the pump. "See? Easy," he said when he returned, and the robo skimmer floated back to its home at the bottom of the pool.

"I'm not too big on the beach. Not too crazy about sailing or boats either," I confessed then told him the story about the summer Leah had taken me to the beach for my fifth birthday. It was the summer we'd gone to collect shells and found a beached dolphin on the shore. The dolphin was still but strangely glistening in the sun, and I'd felt an overwhelming sadness. It was also the summer I'd seen my reflection in the tide pool and realized, for the first time, that I looked nothing like Leah.

"Guess I'm just used to being near water and the ocean. My dad was a pilot in the Navy," he recounted. "He flew missions from an aircraft carrier. He's never actually said it, but I know he was disappointed when I didn't enlist in the Navy."

"I know about dads and disappointments."

Aiden's eyes were even bluer near the water, and all of a sudden the pool looked inviting, cool. I bent down to touch the water with my fingertips.

Then I scooped up a handful of water and flung it in Aiden's direction. He laughed and unbuttoned his shirt, making a cannonball run into the deep end.

"Come on in!" he called out when he surfaced.

I could see his legs slap the water in a fast crawl. In the water, everything was movement, even the reflection of the palm trees surrounding the pool, their trunks spiraling around like a double helix of DNA. I took off my cover-up and waded in from the steps, hanging on to the side of the pool, but the water felt good, soft and safe. I let go of the side and floated on my back. There was nothing but the brightness of the sky, and I closed my eyes and let the water take me wherever it wanted. All those forgotten swim lessons came back to me, and I turned over and swam across the pool to Aiden.

"Race you?" I asked.

He looked surprised.

He was the stronger swimmer, but it didn't matter as

I pushed off the wall. Submerged, I held my breath, weightless, and glided through the water. Bubbles and water slipped past my skin, until I came out of the water to breathe, my arms slicing the water. Aiden surfaced first, and when I reached him I cupped my hands around his face. It was the perfect place to ask him, the ideal opportunity to ask him about the baby car seat, his hands around my waist, but I knew his answer could change everything, and I didn't want to hear it, not then, not there.

I kissed his lips instead, and he kissed me back. His lips, his tongue, tasted so good, water and salt, and I sank down with him. Submerged in the water, I wanted more than his kisses. I wanted to feel his chest against mine, his thighs wrapped around me, and he held me like that at first, then gently, he slowly pulled away. And there was only the soft caress of water on my body when we came up for air.

January 6, 2008

Dear Alex—

Out on deck, I watch the swells rise up with the southerly winds. There's less than one hundred meters of visibility today, and I suddenly remember the dream I had last night. I was back in my room under the gable in our old house, and it felt good to see it again, the white clapboard, even if only in a dream. I haven't thought about the house for a long time. Those Cape Cod-style houses were originally built to withstand New England's stormy weather, but our cottage in Redondo Beach couldn't bear up after you were gone, and Mom and Dad sold it a few years ago, moving into a small apartment. Then they decided to move back to Boston. They are okay and not. They are the same and not.

Jack goes to visit them every couple of months. Mom still buys lotto tickets every Friday, not because she thinks she'll win, but because she knows she won't. I think it's her way of arguing with chance, embracing the slim probabilities of winning and the unlikely odds that she would outlive her youngest son.

Dad is Dad. I worry about him, though. He tries to put up a good front. It's his way not to talk about things, about what happened to you. He likes his volunteer work with the VA, and the class he teaches at the junior college. But I saw him once at the new house in Boston, after his old Navy buddies had left. He sent Mom to bed then collected all the wine and beer glasses and lined them up on the kitchen counter. Then he drank up the leftovers in each glass, one by one.

In our old house our bedrooms weren't connected, but in my dream they opened up into each other. I saw your desk and your books and the lamp on your nightstand. I touched each one, but couldn't feel them. But I could feel you, and it hit me, in my dream, that the absence of something, of someone, can be more tangible then something that exists in the physical world.

Above your desk, pages were tacked onto a bulletin board, but I couldn't see what was written. They were flapping like flags in a wind. Then I moved closer, and saw they were pages with columns of numbers running up and down. It took me another minute to understand, and then I realized. The pages had been lifted from an almanac, and the columns showed the precise times of sunrise and sunset for every day of the calendar year.

Al – ways –
Aiden

CHAPTER 15

AIDEN WAS WAITING IN HIS CAR OUTSIDE MY house, the engine running. When I got in, I turned around to look in the back. There was a jumble of slick diving gear, oxygen tanks and wetsuits, and rubbery flippers, but there was no car seat. He was wearing black Converse today, and one of his shoelaces was untied, I noticed. But somehow it didn't look like an oversight, more like he was testing out different options.

It was the first time I was in his car, surrounded by his things, and I wanted to take all of it in, absorb everything. There was the change he kept at the bottom of the cup holder, the CDs wedged into the driver door pocket, a torn-off page of a daily desk calendar with today's date—August 1, and *Moby Dick* on the car floor.

It wasn't a far drive to the movie theater, but I noticed right off that he was a cautious driver. He didn't just slow down, but stopped completely at every stop sign, and was attentive to the road and other drivers.

"You drive like a grandma," I joked, but he didn't laugh. He turned and planted a kiss on my forehead.

"I'm just a careful driver. Nothing wrong with that, right?"

"Right."

He brought the book with him to the movie theater. We were a little early to the screening, so we went to the café that was tucked away in the lobby. He put the book on our table and poured cream into his coffee. The cream came out pure white, a little thick, reminding me of the glues and pastes, acrylic mediums and glosses I'd experimented with for my collages. They turned the paper transparent, joining two images together, like overlays.

"You're going to love it," he said, excited about seeing a film that was part of a retrospective of 1960s film directors. The film was *Breathless,* a classic black and white film by renegade French film director Jean Luc Goddard, he told me.

He picked up a piece of paper from the floor. "Did you see this?" Someone had scribbled *extract the secrets of my soul* on the bottom of a theater handout, he pointed out to me, handing me the paper. "Funny, huh? Almost like a subtitle."

"Secrets and subtitles? An interesting combination."

Twilight was settling in from the panorama window facing the freeway and our table and the book lit up with the last rays of sunset. "Okay, so what's the real story about . . . *this* book?" I asked.

"Ah. *This* book. *Moby Dick* is kind of helping me figure something out."

"Figure what out?"

"It's complicated, and I want to explain it all to you, really I do," he said, his voice dropping low. "And I will, I promise, but it's a crossroads for me and I don't want to mess up. Most of all, I don't want to be afraid."

"Crossroads?" I heard the echo of Miles's voice. "Afraid of what?" He was talking in riddles and they were making me dizzy, as though I'd just scaled an eight-foot wall. "All right. I like the occasional brainteaser," I tried again. "But tell me again, why *Moby Dick*, of all books?"

He looked up at me as though I should know.

But I didn't. Aiden was like the Polaroid film I'd found only a few months ago. Leah had been on a short-lived cleaning tear and had thrown away her old Polaroid camera and a bunch of old film, but I retrieved it from the trash, curious about the old-school instant camera. I took a few shots and kept going. The camera would spit out the strange, square photos in minutes. But when the novelty of that wore off, I experimented with how to separate the photo paper from the throwaway backing. With the backing off, the runny emulsion was still wet and pliable. Later, I tested transferring the image onto paper usually used for pastels. This kind of paper had an irregular texture pressed into the surface, and I messed it up when I did it too quickly. Finally, I repeated the experiment, taking it slow, and the images appeared, unpredictable, but worth the wait.

"Maddie?" Aiden asked, tracing my name with his fingertip, lightly on my arm.

"What?" I folded up the paper and stuffed it in my purse. Even jammed down at the bottom of my bag, I could feel it wrapping around me.

He hooked his finger into the back loop of my jeans and pulled me close. Suddenly his face went deadly serious. "I have something I want to show you," he said, and he picked up the book and handed it to me. "Here."

In my hands, the book was light, almost weightless. Even though I wasn't much of a reader, every book was full of numbers, and that's what I looked for first. I opened it up and examined it. It was 543 pages long, with 135 chapters, an old Signet classic paperback from 1961.

"You'd like chapter 103," he said. "It's all about measurements of the whale's skeleton." He took the book back from me and opened it up, reading me a passage about the dimensions of the ninety-ton whale, eighty-five feet in length and forty feet in circumference. When he read, I could imagine it, the whale in all its length and weight, all the numbers that described its mammoth size.

"So why this book?"

"It helped me before, and I'm hoping it will help me again."

"Help you with what?"

He stopped to take a long gulp of air. "I've been wanting to tell you, but it's not something you can just tell someone right away."

"What is it?" I asked, and I felt the weight of the book, the moment, the length of time in hours, in days, in minutes it had taken for Aiden to finally tell me.

"There was a woman . . . and . . . and she had my baby."

"A woman?"

"It was just one night . . . I can't describe it . . . it was this one crazy night . . . like a dream. We were on a ship. I was a volunteer for Greenpeace on a mission to save whales. The woman's name is Olivia . . . and the baby was . . . we weren't careful, and it was . . . a mistake."

"A mistake?"

I was trying to take all this in, to wrap my head around everything he was telling me. A woman, a baby, a ship, and whales, seemed such an unlikely combination of words, but I could see by his expression that there was more. "And now . . . I have to figure it out"

"Figure what out?"

"Whether to give the baby up."

"Give the baby up?"

"Olivia wants us to give the baby up for adoption."

The hardest silence fell between us, like some sappy movie, a long pause in a bad soap opera.

I had to repeat it, even though he knew. I had to say it again so he'd understand. I wanted to say the words slowly, quietly, but they came out loud, like a dare.

"I'm adopted."

He looked at me. "I know. And I would have known even if you hadn't told me."

My words came out softly this time. "Adoption is a word most people misunderstand. It's not just about parents adopting a child. It's also about a child adopting the parents and the world they live in. If someone else, someone other than my artist mom or my engineer dad had adopted me would I have ever been interested in math or art?"

He shook his head. "I don't know, Maddie. I just don't know. Here I am, twenty-two years old, and I have to make a decision like this? If I hadn't made that one mistake, if I hadn't been careless that one night . . ."

I looked at Aiden.

This is why you pull away from me.

All I wanted to do was curl up against him.

His phone rang, and he stood up. "Sorry, Maddie, it's important. I have to take this," he said, stepping away.

"Go ahead," I said, half relieved to have a moment to compose myself.

I picked up Aiden's book and flipped through the pages. This time I noticed the spine was taped up, many of the pages dog-eared, and on the first page, across from a sketch of Herman Melville, was a name scrawled in boyish handwriting on the top right hand corner of the page—Alex.

"I need more time," I heard Aiden say, ending his phone conversation.

I needed time too, to sort things out, piece it all together, but my head was buzzing. Out on the freeway, traffic on one side had come to a complete halt, the sky darkening.

Aiden came back and handed the tickets to an attendant, and I was happy the film was playing in the farthest screening room, far away from the crowds of other moviegoers. It had already started, and Aiden took my hand and led me up the hallway and up to the seats, the floor dotted with tiny, orange pricks of lights. Inside the small theater there were only a few people, and Aiden chose two seats on the last row, precisely in the middle, under the three projection windows. He put his arm around me and I nestled closer. I'd never seen the film before, but I could tell that Aiden knew every scene. I felt his warm body next to me lean forward just a little, seconds before each important moment.

Paris is in black and white.

The boulevards and buildings were wrapped up as if in a package of inky newspaper. Above me, I could see the round eye of the projector, the tiny, three-inch lens shooting images across the room. And in that moment everything made sense, in the center of the dark theater, in Aiden's arms, the flash of subtitles across the screen, with Jean Seberg in her pixie haircut and Jean Paul Belmondo shirtless and chain smoking in a hat in bed, and me, breathless.

January 7, 2008

Dear Alex—

The whale hunter ships have a critical advantage over us.
Unlike them, we can't refuel by tanker mid-sea, and we're
almost halfway through our two-week search for the
hunter ships. Both fuel and time run out very quickly out
here, every minute is crucial and can't be wasted. I take
my turn watching the blips on the radar screen and keeping
watch with binoculars. Fire on a ship can mean disaster,
and yesterday we had another in a series of fire drills. And
with each new day I'm feeling stronger and better prepared
for what is to come.

 This morning, I fix my camera on a tripod. It feels
good to let the camera stand on its own, steady and apart
from me. I'm trying out time-lapse photography of the
Southern Ocean sky, and the camera will record without
my interruption or input in various locations on the ship,
the bridge windows, at the edge of the prow, to catch the
moving shadows. Sometime later I'll stitch the frames
together to speed up time, reinventing the view, so that the
clouds will streak fast across the sky.

 Hours later I begin to unbolt the camera, and Olivia
appears on deck. She kneels down with me to help me pack
up the equipment. She unscrews the lens for me and lifts
up each lever of the tripod leg locks, ably collapsing them
and shrinking their length. I look at her and the open deck
becomes my confessional, stripping away my artifice, every
trick I've played in order to live with myself. I tell Olivia

about you. I tell her everything that happened on that day, and everything that should have happened, and she listens without saying a word, without judgment. Every detail spills out of me with the force of water gushing from a dam, and she holds me.

I'm relieved when we're interrupted by a shipmate.

He says it's our turn for more inflatable boat exercises. The water in the Southern Ocean can be less than zero degrees, and everyone needs to continue to train. We wear reddish orange waterproof jumpsuits, equipped with knives and whistles for emergencies, and helmets that are insulated. Any fall into the water can be life threatening and practice is key.

Each one of us learns how to operate the radio, and the engine controls on every inflatable, getting a feel for the steering and the characteristics of each boat, and understanding how to launch and retrieve the boat from our ship.

It's all part of the endgame, to do what needs to be done for the mission, to hunt down the hunters and drive them away.

Al – ways –
Aiden

CHAPTER 16

PULLED INTO THE PARKING SPACE IN BACK OF TWAINS, but kept the engine and AC going for another five minutes, trying to cool off before meeting Aiden. He was already waiting for me, sitting at our booth when I walked in, but I noticed there were three menus on the table instead of two.

"Olivia just called me. She's coming."

"What? Coming here?"

"Yes."

"Now? But . . ."

"It's a good opportunity for you to meet Olivia, right?"

My brain was in a knot and my heart started to pound. I took a deep breath. I picked up one of the laminated menus, flipped it open then closed it up, putting it down again when a woman blew in from the door.

A flash of long, copper-red hair.

She came in quickly, heading directly to Aiden like a missile. I was so focused on Olivia's face I didn't see at first what she was holding in both hands. When she reached Aiden, I could see it clearly. It was the car seat. Olivia let it go, and it dropped with a loud thud on the floor.

"If you're going to take her out this afternoon, you're going to need this. "She's at my friend's house now." Aiden opened his mouth to say something to her, but I saw the words dry up in his mouth.

I'd imagined she'd be tall, like Aiden, but she was tiny. She stood like a dancer, erect, her feet turned out, and I felt big and clunky next to her. And she was beautiful, only the tiniest of freckles dotting her eggshell complexion.

"Who's this?" she asked Aiden, turning to me, and I braced myself for a confrontation, but there was none.

"This is Maddie."

"Oh, okay, hi," Olivia sighed then suddenly smiled, and she looked at me as though she remembered something. "Aiden told me you're an artist, right?"

"Yes," I answered.

"Sit down. We can talk," Aiden said to Olivia.

"I can't stay. And I'm so tired of talking, Aiden . . . I can't talk anymore . . . really there's nothing else to talk . . . about," she said, her voice dissipating with each word. "I'm going back to Canada in a few days. I only came to L.A. so you could spend more time with her and make up your mind."

"Olivia, please," Aiden attempted again.

"All I need from you is your answer and soon."

Olivia looked at me. She wasn't that much older than Aiden, but her eyes looked sad, like they'd seen a million sunsets. "You see, Aiden. What I told you came true."

"I know you'll help Aiden do the right thing," she said to me. "Because you're the one." She then turned around and left.

It had happened so fast, Olivia's coming, her going, I wasn't even sure I'd actually seen her. It couldn't have been more than a minute and she'd evaporated. But there it was, the car seat, pretty and pastel, its cushiony lining, proof. The two ends of the seat buckle dangled heavily down to the floor and I felt my arms go limp too.

Wobbly, I tried to get up, but Aiden reached out to me before I could take a step. "Maddie, don't leave, please," he said, his voice shaky.

"I don't know if I can do this," I said, my brain in free-fall. Everything in the coffee shop, the booths, the tiles, and the carpet was a mush of brown, brown and tan, ochre and rust, sepia and sienna, no bright spot of color.

"Don't go," he begged, reaching for my hand. "This has nothing to do with you and me, with us."

"What are you talking about? Of course it does. It has everything to do with us."

I could see he was trying to piece it all together in his head, and I wished my hands would stop trembling.

"But you and me . . . has nothing to do with *her*."

"Stop saying that."

I saw the blaze of red hair again in my head and her dainty feet. Still hanging on to my wrist, Aiden looked broken apart.

My mind swirled dizzily. "Something you said before . . . the other day. I didn't understand. What did you mean when you said you would have known I was adopted even if I hadn't told you?"

Aiden seemed relieved by my completely random question. "It's the way you look at people and things, as though you're looking for their derivations."

Derivations? In math, a derivative was the instantaneous rate of change or slope of a function, but a derivation could also mean the source or origin of something. "I'm not really following."

"You always seem to look for origins, for where people and things come from." Aiden let go of my wrist and took my hand.

"How would you know that?"

"That day, near the fountain, literally just before you told me you were adopted, you looked down at a bottle cap embedded in the cement. And I could tell, you were wondering how it got there, and whether someone put it there on purpose, to be found."

"You noticed that?"

"Of course. I knew right away that you look for the beginnings of everything. The beginnings of everything except yourself."

"Except myself?" It was my own fault I'd steered

himself away from the subject. "Never mind about me. What about your baby?"

He looked at me, but didn't answer. Three people were lined up at the aged cash register, and the change tray popped out and rang loudly.

"What about your baby?"

"Olivia's already decided. She's going back to campaigning, back to the sea. That's what she does. She's not a bad person, but campaigning is her whole life, and a baby, a child, being a full-time mother, just doesn't figure into it. At first, she thought she could do it, be a full-time mother, but now she changed her mind. She thinks the baby would be better off with a family and she's set on giving the baby up for adoption, and now I'm the only one who can decide . . . whether I keep the baby . . . or not."

Looking rumpled, Aiden pressed his lips just above my ear. "I don't want to say it one day," Aiden whispered.

I felt his sweet breath on my face.

"What don't you want to say?"

"I don't want to look back one day and say I made the wrong decision. I don't want to say I was too late."

January 9, 2008

Dear Alex—

*I can feel the mood on the ship shifting. The wind meter
points to NNW and we're closing in on our showdown with
the Japanese ship. It's not just a whaling ship but also an
enormous whale meat factory on the move, equipped for
processing what they kill. It's out there, close. We can
almost feel its presence. Although there's no real night,
there's fog, and when the fog lifts we'll see what the radar
screen shows us, the hunter ship, spotted first as a blip in
the early hours of the morning, and forcing us to change
our course. We will become the hunter ship's shadow.*

*There's a collective gearing up for what's to come, and
there's a new restlessness and adrenaline-fueled energy in
the cold air, but anticipation keeps us warm for tomorrow.
Supplies are being loaded up on the inflatable boats.*

*The inflatable boats are called RIBs, short for Rigid
Inflatable Boats. Below the water they're a hard fiberglass
that allows the boat to travel at high speeds even through
rough seas. There's a specially constructed rubber tube that
runs along the bow and sides of the hull that gives it
buoyancy and stability in water, but nothing that can harm
the whales.*

*Our RIB is eight meters in length and can travel great
distances. It can carry up to eighteen people and a hundred
gallons of fuel, and can store fresh food and dry clothes.*

We are at full throttle, and the chase is on tomorrow.

*After midnight I wake up in my bed, the rest of my
berth mates gone, but Olivia's there, sitting by my side.*

She's cold, her tiny hands icy, but her face is flushed. She's crying and she won't tell me why. She only says that she too has regrets and a promise she must keep.

I listen and then she tells me that whatever happens this night or tomorrow, she wants me to know that she's bound to the ocean and the sky. It's the earth that's both her soul mate and her child. She cries again, and this time her tears are her apology.

Tomorrow, we'll put our bodies between the whales and the harpoons of the Japanese whaling ship, the Nisshun Maru, and tonight I banish all caution and I reach out and pull Olivia to me, inside the cocoon of my narrow berth, my messy sheets and blankets.

Al – ways –
Aiden

CHAPTER 17

I PRESSED HARD ON THE ACCELERATOR AS I SPED through a succession of yellow lights. I was almost at Jack's house when, too late, I noticed the sign—photo enforced—and a flash of light came off the red-light camera. I was beginning to believe in omens.

The house was small, two-stories and dwarfed by a giant California oak that stood towering over the front lawn. Two rows of old rose bushes lined the curvy stone path to the front door. It was one of those odd Valley 1940s houses, where the front door was offset but the house itself looked freshly painted, white roses still blooming despite the summer's heat. I walked up the three steps then turned left to ring the bell. Aiden came to the door wearing a rumpled T-shirt and cargo pants.

Inside, everything was neat, furnished with colorful Kilim rugs and rattan furniture. In the corner of the living room, pristine, was a triptych of computer screens, with two long keyboards below and a pair of speakers. The screens were dark, but I moved in closer to get a better look, running my hand across the top of one of the screens.

I turned to Aiden, but before I could ask, he explained. Jack was helping him out with a short film he was working on.

"*Your* film?"

"Yes. The raw footage from the ship."

"Can I see it?"

"Nothing to see yet. I haven't been able to work on it," Aiden replied, and he took both my hands and pulled me gently away from the screens. "Anyway, Jack's run out of ice. Let's get out of here and get something cold to drink," Aiden hurriedly proposed. "I have a photo idea for you."

"What idea?"

"You'll see."

I wanted to stay and see the rest of the house, but most of all the colors of his bedroom. I imagined shades of celadon and cerulean blue, but Aiden was insistent, and he led me out the front door.

He jumped into my passenger seat and adjusted all the air vents. His face was flushed from heat, his T-shirt clinging to his back. He ran his hand through his hair and looked like he hadn't slept all night.

"You just missed it," he said, as I drove by. "Looks like you're going to have to turn around."

When I backtracked, I realized the place was hidden away between a tired-looking market and a Rite Aid pharmacy. "It looks like a walk-up and drive-thru. Probably no indoor seating."

"And probably no AC. But that's okay."

I slowed down near the drive-thru, scouring the lot for a parking space, and a car honked impatiently behind us.

"I hate bad drivers," Aiden said.

I finally found a parking space and we stood in line at the tinted walk-up window, which opened up and then closed with each customer. Inside was a guy with a pierced chin and a headphone and across from him, an identical window for the drive-thru customers.

A heavy-set man standing in line was wearing a black undershirt, with a tiger tattoo on his right shoulder. He was so big I didn't notice the little girl standing alongside him.

"I'm thirsty, Daddy," she said to the man with the tattoo. She was wearing a strange combo of gem-studded ballet slippers and a baseball uniform. Her hair was messy, uncombed, as though she'd just tumbled out of bed.

"I only have enough for my coffee," the guy grumbled at her. "I'll buy you something else later."

"But I'm thirsty now," she whimpered, and Aiden looked at me.

"What kind of a father thinks only about his own coffee?" Aiden whispered to me.

Aiden ordered fries and a drink, and we sat down under one of three canvas umbrellas. I looked up and saw a pair of sea gulls on the roof.

"Strange, right?" Aiden said. "Seagulls in the middle

of the valley. That's why I brought you here, but we have to wait a little."

I picked up a pen and napkin someone had left on the table and tried to sketch a couple standing in line. I attempted to capture the shape of their heads against the sky as they stood close together, but after I was done, the drawing looked sloppy and I crumpled it up. Who was I kidding? This was pointless. Next, I took out my camera and snapped a photo of the same couple. At least I could press a simple camera button. I took the shot from behind, two figures in shadow, the guy's arm intertwined with the girl's.

The battery sign of my camera started to blink and I shut the camera off. Aiden too looked as though he was in power saving mode.

"She did it. She signed off on the adoption papers yesterday," Aiden suddenly said.

"So, now it's up to you to . . ." I stopped myself from finishing the sentence.

"Not everyone should be a father. Case in point, our tattooed father-of-the-year example," he said, his eyes troubled.

"But some people are."

"I thought you, of all people, would understand."

"I do and I don't. What does your holy *Moby Dick* say about it?" I flung out, immediately regretting it.

Aiden looked at me strangely, and I thought he was going to be mad, but he didn't react to my provocation.

"The word 'father' appears twenty-seven times in the book," he said calmly instead.

"You counted them?"

"No," he explained. "It's a search function on a website I found."

"I see," I said, but I didn't want to talk about that book anymore.

"Look, Maddie, I'm supposed to sign off on the adoption papers . . . and soon."

"I know."

He stopped talking, and the street became eerily silent, as though someone had pressed pause, and the silence seemed to drag on forever. "Are you okay?" I asked.

Another pair of sea gulls landed on the roof and Aiden suddenly came back to life.

"They're here. Take out your camera, Maddie. This is it, my idea to help you."

"What?"

"Think of it as a creative jumpstart," and Aiden started throwing the fries up on top of the umbrellas. The gulls swooped down. "Take the shots now," he said, and I started snapping away, the gulls in motion, their wings in flight. I couldn't stop, and I kept taking photos until my battery completely died.

"The afternoon light was perfect," Aiden said when I was done. "Like cameo lighting."

"Cameo?"

"It's where a single light focuses on one person in a

scene," he explained. "Come to think of it, it all makes sense now. Meeting you," he said, looking up, "There was a special light, the first time I saw you. In some movies, it's all about the light," he said, excited now. "Huston was brilliant, the way he used light and darkness in *Moby Dick*. But the casting was all off. Gregory Peck played crazy Captain Ahab. He should have played Starbuck, the hero of the story," Aiden said. "Maddie?"

Behind him, the sun fired up a red convertible waiting in the drive-through line, and the ground seemed to shift.

"I'm sorry I've been kind of a mess today. You've been so great."

Aiden stood up and pulled me to him, and the asphalt felt soft under my feet. I leaned against his chest, his arms around me and I closed my eyes. His hands hesitated on my waist then slowly make their way up to my face. He kissed me, first on my forehead, and then on the mouth. His lips landed so softly, and he pulled me in closer. I kissed him back, my mouth lingering on his and in the long and rainless Los Angeles summer there was a different kind of rain inside me. It was a downpour.

CHAPTER 18

AIDEN SPENT THE REST OF THE DAY WITH OLIVIA and the baby, and I was glad I had a night drill. We wore goggles and a dust mask, along with a reflective safety vest and heavy work gloves. We were doing a search-and-rescue drill. It was pitch black and we had only our flashlights to guide us.

My walkie-talkie crackled with voices.

Partial collapse, five injured outside.

The incident commander sent us to walk around the perimeter of the house that had been set up for the earthquake drill, looking for fallen power lines and trees. Even if there were no collapsed walls, we knew to look for any large cracks. I found one on the south side of the house. It started from the foundation and zigzagged up to the windowsill, and I called it in.

Then we broke up into two-person teams and Angela and I were sent to locate and shut off the gas and power. In the dark, the gas valve, normally coming out of a ground pipe and at the gas meter, was hard to find. When I did, I took a wrench and tried to turn the main valve as we'd been instructed, but the valve wouldn't budge.

I tried again, this time using both my hands, and it worked. Then we moved on to the electrical breaker box on the other side of the drill house. I opened the metal door, turned off all the small breakers first, then shut off the main.

From there we went to the front door, on which another team member had already taped a bright yellow paper, and outlined a rectangular box with a diagonal slash. This was a sign to let others know that there was already someone searching the structure.

We made our way slowly through the house. "Remember the left hand rule," my team leader reiterated behind me. I put my left hand on the wall, moving forward, never taking my hand off the wall as I walked through the structure.

I remembered the instructions we were given.

Smell for gas. Listen for leaks and voices.

Get debris out of the way, but watch out for power cords still possibly charged.

Touch a door only with the back of your hand to see if it's hot.

Look out for small children and animals hiding in closets, under beds, and in cupboards.

"Observe and report only," the liaison officer said on the walkie-talkie.

"All clear," I reported.

But then I walked into a back bedroom. The TV was on the floor, smashed. Books and clothing were strewn everywhere. I knew the house was unoccupied, but I was sure I heard a sound. I stopped and listened for the sound again. I bent down and aimed my flashlight under the bed. I saw something run across the room, then out the window.

Blacker than the night, is a cat.

Left behind, is a litter of two, tiny charcoal kittens.

I called in what I'd found.

"Observe and report *only*, Maddie," a voice ordered me on the walkie-talkie.

I looked at Angela. We followed the others back outside, but the two of us came back when everyone had left to go home. We gathered up the kittens in our arms, hid them under our jackets, and Angela brought them home to her house.

CHAPTER 19

THE NEXT MORNING, I REMEMBERED A NEW dream. I was floating underwater, suspended in a sea of green. Holding my breath, I swam upward toward a beam of light, to what I thought was the surface, but instead, the rocky bottom loomed up at me in a swirling eddy. When I realized my mistake, it was too late, and I was caught in a moving mass of kelp that surrounded me, pulling me down deeper and deeper. Just then, as my lungs were about to burst, the sounds of a text message intruded, waking me up.

Bryn?

I sat up in bed too fast, and my head swirled madly. I had to lie back down again before I could look at my cell screen. No. She was still MIA. It was just a text from my manager about a shift change.

I took my time getting out of bed, slowly this time, and made my way to the window. Outside, the sky was painted with weird streaks of white. Some people called it "earthquake weather." But Miles would have said there was absolutely no scientific connection between weather and earthquakes, a geologic process that could happen at any time, in all climate zones, and any weather conditions. Still, I was uneasy. In the shower, I turned both faucets on full blast, and the rush of tepid water felt good. I washed my hair and again, took my time, but I was still a little unsteady, and I avoided looking down at the drain. I was determined, though. No bad dream, no text, no woozy shower was going to ruin the memory of Aiden's kiss. Grabbing a small carton of orange juice from the fridge, I downed it in two gulps.

Leah came into the kitchen from the back door with a couple of bags of groceries. She was planning an impromptu good-bye party for one of our old adoption support group members, who was going to Korea to find his birth mother, she said, as she started to unpack. Then she looked at me and reached over to tuck a wet, wayward hair behind my ear.

"How's that CERT class going?" She asked.

"It's great. Challenging, but great."

"I'm glad for you. I'm glad you're doing it," she said. Leah paused for a moment. "I think . . . I'll make it a barbecue," Leah said. "What do you think?"

"I think this birth mother pilgrimage is a bad idea. It probably won't end well."

"But it might," Leah said then started to go over the guest list. I was only half listening when Leah blurted out something else. She had spoken to my birthparents,

Alma and Rafael, she said, and they were thinking of moving to New York.

"What did you say?"

My stomach began to boil and the bright aqua kitchen cabinets melted into an ugly, moss green.

"I told them you're going to art school there."

"You told them about art school, about New York? Why did you do that? Why should they know anything about me?"

A year ago, Leah had told me that Alma and Rafael were applying for visas to the States, but I'd deliberately put it out of my mind. Now it was there, this giant crack in the adoption wall, an opening so big I couldn't ignore it.

"Don't be upset, Maddie. Maybe it would do you some good to write to them," Leah said calmly.

"I've told you before. No. They have no rights to me or my life."

"Don't do it for them. Do it for you."

I stormed out of the kitchen and stood at the bottom of the stairs holding on to the railing. If only I could talk with Bryn.

But talking to Bryn wasn't happening, and I went back upstairs and pulled out Bryn's pomegranate T-shirt from my top drawer. I wadded up the T-shirt and came down the stairs, then stuffed it in the large clothing bag Leah kept in the laundry room off the kitchen for Goodwill. Good riddance.

The groceries were still half unpacked in the kitchen,

but Leah was nowhere in sight. I made myself a sandwich, took another juice from the fridge, and headed off to work. On my way out of the house I passed through the garage, knocking over a cardboard box and dislodging it. There, wedged between the box and the floor, was one of Jordan's old slap tags. Long ago, Leah had gone through the house and garage with a fine tooth comb, getting rid of anything remotely related to Jordan's gang, but they must have missed this lone slap tag. Holding it in my hand, a wave of nausea rolled over me. There was nowhere to throw it so I shoved it down into the bottom of my jeans pocket.

A long two hours later, I grabbed a black coffee, some sugar packets, and the sandwich I'd brought for lunch, taking my half-hour lunch break outside at one of the wrought iron tables under the supermarket overhang. I took a couple of bites of the sandwich, but it was soggy. Out in the parking lot, the stock guy in his neon yellow vest was gathering up the scattered shopping carts and returning them in a long, caterpillar-like line. The carts clattered as he maneuvered them across the parking lot, and for some reason I shivered in the heat.

Aiden sneaked up from behind me and kissed the top of my head. I turned around, reaching for his hands and saw he was all decked out, dark brown, lace-up shoes and a white, collared shirt. His pants had a neatly ironed crease, and he was wearing a tie. But his hands were clammy.

"Where are you going, all dressed up?"

"I'm going to talk to a lawyer."

"Oh." A small panic fluttered in my stomach. "A lawyer?"

"No, I haven't decided yet, if that's what you're thinking."

He leaned over and picked up the two sugar packets I'd left unopened on the table. "Sugar packet football," he announced.

"What?"

"It's a game."

"Not in the mood for games today," and I pushed away my coffee and half-eaten tuna sandwich.

"Come on. I'll teach you."

I lost the first three rounds, all my packets falling hopelessly to the floor. But after a few more tries, I finally got the hang of it, exerting just the right amount of thrust to win the next five.

"Guess I just kicked your butt."

"You sure did. You learn fast," he said, grinning and lobbing the packet playfully at me. "Feeling better?"

I was. I caught the packet. "Where did you learn this game?"

"I don't know. Something I picked up somewhere, I guess."

"Where?"

"On the ship." I waited a moment before I asked. "That ship? When exactly were you on that ship?"

"January of 2008. Two weeks."

"I still don't exactly get it, the *Moby Dick* thing."

"You have to read it to get it. It's about ambiguities and the decisions we make, idealism versus pragmatism, right versus wrong. But I think it's really about wanting what you're afraid of and fearing what you want. I've been wanting to give this to you," Aiden said, and he took the book out from his blazer pocket and carefully tore a page from it.

"What are you doing?" The sound of him tearing it out gave me a jolt.

"Maybe you can use it . . . in one of your collages."

"Are you sure?"

"Here, please take it," he said, putting the torn page on my lap.

I didn't know what to say. "I can't do it."

"Can't do what?" Aiden asked.

"My birthparents are thinking of moving to New York. And they called my mother."

"They called your mom?"

"All three of us had open adoptions. We even went down to Guatemala . . . once," I explained. "My mom's been writing and sending photos to all our birthparents for years."

"And you?"

"I don't write."

"Why not?" he asked.

"I just don't."

"You mean you know who they are, and you've never written back to them?" He asked, leaning forward as though I was some litmus test for how things could work out for him and his baby.

"No."

He watched me closely now. "Really?"

"That's it. I can't do it. I can't go to New York, not with *them* possibly there."

"Melville lived in New York, near the Battery," Aiden said. "He grew up right at the bottom tip of Manhattan, where he could see the sea birds and ships."

Tears started to well up in my eyes. "I'm telling you how I feel, and you're giving me Melville's bio?"

"I'm sorry, I didn't mean to be unsympathetic," he said, and reached for my hand. "But think of it, Maddie, New York's a big city. You wouldn't have to see them, and what are the chances of you bumping into them? Almost nil. You have a better chance of winning the lottery."

"But you don't understand."

"Understand what?"

"It's ridiculous really, but sometimes I think it's true."

"What's true?"

"That my mom had wanted an open adoption, and that she'd kept up with our birthparents all these years not because of some New-Age adoption philosophy, but because she didn't really want us, me, all to herself. Like an adoption escape hatch."

Aiden gathered me up in his arms, and I told him about the time we all went to New York.

"It was supposed to have been a vacation for the five

of us, but Jordan was in Juvenile Hall, his first time. It was my mom who insisted we go anyway, that my dad needed a family vacation.

"At first, the city seemed so big to me, with its miles of pavement and the sounds of the subway below and the taxis and buses. But I liked the logic of the grid of numbered streets, from East 1st Street in Lower Manhattan to the tip of the island on West 220th Street. Miles had given me a map of the city, but I'd felt as though I didn't need it, that the numbers told me exactly where I was.

"I wanted to see the Planetarium. The eighty-seven-foot diameter sphere, boxed like a gift in an acre of glass, took my breath away, and the sloping walkway through thirteen billion years of time, but the laser show made me cold and dizzy. I started to panic and then cry, the lights playing tricks on my eyes. My dad told me to close my eyes, that it would help me regain my balance and it did, but when we got out, my mom made us stand in front of the entrance to take a picture—to send to our birthparents, she said. I didn't understand why she would do that, include *them* in our trip, in *our family* vacation."

Aiden looked at me. "I get it, now. I understand."

"So . . . How old is your baby?"

Aiden blinked at me. "She's about ten months," and I couldn't help myself, calculating back, adding ten months to nine months, all leading back to early January 2008. "She's with Olivia today. But Olivia's going back to Canada in a couple of days and she's been talking with a married cousin of hers there who wants to adopt her," he said. "Here's a picture." He pulled out a small photo from his wallet. "I took it an hour after she was born."

"Really?"

"I flew up there . . . when she was born, up in Toronto."

"You were there?"

I looked at the photograph, the tiny, newborn face in a pink cap.

"It was like a lightning bolt inside of me the minute I saw her. I'd never seen anything so perfect.

"Then how can you think of giving her up?"

Aiden looked at me and shifted in his seat. "I want to do what's best for her. And even with everything you've told me, you turned out okay, didn't you?"

His question sent pinpricks up my arms and legs. I tried to take a breath, but every bit of air seemed to be squeezed out of my lungs. I hadn't told Aiden I'd bought my own copy of *Moby Dick*, that I'd been secretly reading it, word by word, to see if there was something I could use, some passage in that book that would convince him not to give up the baby.

Suddenly there was a little vibration, a quick tiny rattle.

"An earthquake?" Aiden asked.

"Could be a semi passing through. But if it was an earthquake, it couldn't be more than a three on the Richter," I speculated calmly.

Aiden looked unnerved. "Felt bigger to me."

"What did you name her?" I asked, with all my strength.

"Her name is Hope."

"Hope," I repeated. "That's a beautiful name."

"Olivia and I decided on it together. But I guess it kind of made perfect sense, because she was conceived on the ship, the *Esperanza.*

"Everything boils down to one thing. All I have to do is sign or not sign, and my entire life changes forever."

"And her life too. I have to go back to work," and I got up from the table, but my feet felt like lead.

"Already?"

Signature Required. It was one of Miles's stupid labels buzzing around in my head. Then I imagined it, a birth certificate, dates and numbers and signatures, and Hope crossed out.

I turned around and grabbed him by the shoulders. "How could giving her up be right? How can you even think of doing that?" I erupted. "Don't you understand?"

I had to sit down again. "Being adopted, however great your new parents are, however wonderful your life turns out to be, it's still a weight you carry around with you your whole life. It's a rejection you never forget." I tried to hold them back, but the tears fell down my cheeks. "Please don't sign, Aiden. Please don't do it."

I felt another vibration under my feet, a little bigger this time, and I knew. Aiden's signature would be a fault line between us, a convergence of the Earth's tectonic plates, an earthquake that would separate us into different landmasses, forever.

January 10, 2008

Dear Alex—

The numbers are hard to believe. Hundreds of thousands of whales have been killed in the last three hundred years. Even the recent commercial whaling ban hasn't stopped the slaughter. They come up with ways to get around the ban, finding loopholes. You were the one who told me this, long ago. You sat up nights reading all the ugly statistics, but I only half listened. Sure, I found the book in a sale bin of the bookstore and gave it to you, but you were the one who read it, inhaled it, every night. The book wasn't some old story for you, some footnote in history, irrelevant. It was the book that lit you up, and you battled Captain Ahab and his demons in your own dreams. I could hear you talking in your sleep trying to both reason and argue with him and with all the captains that came before and after him.

Dad and I packed up all the things in your room. Mom couldn't do it. We gave a lot away, your clothes, your books, your games. Dad asked me if I wanted anything to remember you by, and there was only one thing I wanted: your book. I put it on a shelf above my desk, but I couldn't open it, let alone read it. For months it gathered dust on the shelf, until one night I dreamt we were on Jack's boat and the book had fallen in the water. You dove in to get it, then climbed back into the boat and gave it to me. In the morning I opened the book and started to read it. I felt your presence in it, in every page, and when I

finished it, days later, I knew what I needed to do, and
that's when I made my promise to you.

Our time is now and this is no dream.

The RIB inflatable is equipped with a water pump and
spray system to frustrate the hunter ships. I'm in the RIB
with Olivia, but there's no time to think about her. There's
no time to think about the night we spent together.

Small and agile, the inflatable boat has a delicate
steering system and can be held just off the bow of the
hunter ship at high speeds and in pack ice. It can aim a
water spray up onto the harpoon deck and the spotter's
towers, causing the hunters to lose sight of the whales and
miss their shots. But the inflatable has very little
protection against the water cannons, barely a windscreen.

We are in full-speed pursuit. They are dead ahead,
and we can hear the loudspeakers with their warnings not
to approach their ship.

Keep away.

Keep away from our ship.

We carry only handwritten placards in bright yellow.
Our placards try to refute the word that's stenciled in
white on their ship, "Research." The word is cynical. The
word is camouflage. There's no research being done on this
ship, no science, only destruction.

And then we hear it. It's the sound of the grenade
tipped harpoon being launched from the ship into the
water.

It makes the most awful of noises.

Al – ways –
Aiden

CHAPTER 20

THE HEAT WASN'T BREAKING. EVEN AT NIGHT, the sidewalks seemed to expand and buckle up. On TV there were nonstop news stories about the dwindling snow pack in the northern Sierras, and interviews with videos of scientists holding measuring sticks in the low snow. Less than half the normal rainfall fell last winter, they reported.

About thirty people showed up for the impromptu good-bye-and-good-luck barbecue Leah had put together. Most of the old adoption support group parents and kids came, as well as Miles's old Boeing team and their wives. My Uncle Phil and Aunt Adele were there too, loaded down with stacks of travel brochures about the floating hotel they'd chosen for their annual vacation. I glanced at my watch. It was just about time for Aiden to arrive and I was excited and nervous about him meeting my family for the first time.

I looked around the house. Everything was the same, all the little parts that made up the house—Miles's wallet and keys on the hall table, his high blood pressure meds in the kitchen, Leah's collection of magnets and lists on the refrigerator. However, Miles had finally mowed the lawn and the lanterns Leah had bought a couple of years ago in Chinatown were strung perfectly across the backyard, all lit up in a fiery red.

No one was missing except Jordan, whom I hadn't seen or heard from since the day we'd met up at the wildlife reserve.

Miles started making veggie burgers and turkey dogs on the black BBQ, and Leah went back and forth from the kitchen to the backyard patio loaded with heaping plates of food. Leah wasn't much of a cook, except for the hearty soups she made in winter, each one in a different colored-enamel pot, like the green stockpot she used for pea soup and the grey one in which she made mushroom barley. But she'd managed to throw together an international menu of Guatemalan, Korean, and American food, which she served buffet-style on the patio.

"Miles, you didn't forget to buy relish?" Leah called out from the kitchen.

"No, Leah. Got everything on your list," Miles replied dutifully, smoke swirling around his head, his old NASA *Need More Space* BBQ apron a little stained but freshly ironed.

It was nice to see them together. My parents were so different, two opposites that the universe had somehow combined by mistake—artist and scientist. But tonight they were completely in step with one another, Leah handing Miles the empty plate just as the burgers were ready to be taken off the fire.

Aiden arrived just as I was getting more drinks from the extra fridge in the garage. I introduced him to Miles first.

"Aiden's father was a Navy pilot," I said, and that was enough to get Miles to huddle with Aiden and talk about Aiden's dad's missions in the Persian Gulf.

But Leah was a different matter. She had a sixth sense for secrets, and an even keener intuition about babies. All her miscarriages had given her a bewildering talent for predicting the sex of the babies of every pregnant woman she encountered on the street.

Leah gave Aiden a hug, then stood back and gave him the Leah once-over and smiled. If she suspected any babies in Aiden's orbit she didn't show it, and I breathed a sigh of relief. I took Aiden's hand and went around introducing him to Gabriela and the other guests.

A few hours later, Leah was still beaming, her party a success. Aiden was helping Miles clean up, and I went up to my bedroom. I pushed the half-closed door open and found Gabriela, in her soccer shorts, sprawled out on my bedroom floor. Gabriela had a yellow, contractor-sized tape measure hooked into the edge of the floorboard, fully extended, and she was jotting down numbers and measurements on a note pad.

"What are you doing?" I asked.

"Mom said I could have your room when you leave," Gabriela said, quickly unlocking the tape, and it snapped back into its case.

"She said that?"

Gabriela fidgeted with the ends of her hair then put it up with the two black ponytail holders she always kept wrapped around her wrist. "Yes."

"I'm not even gone yet, and she's giving away my room?"

"I didn't mean anything, Maddie."

"Good move, little sister," I blurted out, snatching the tape measure from the floor. "I'm not gone yet."

Gabriela looked up at me. "I swear I wouldn't have done it if I knew you'd get so mad," Gabriela said then bolted, crying, out of the room.

I shut the bedroom door and looked around. On my desk was a photo of Gabriela and me at her first soccer match. I'd taught her how to kick a soccer ball, and pulled out the bed sheets from the linen closet to make tent cities in the living room for her and her friends.

"Maddie?" Gabriela opened the door a crack. "I'm sorry."

I walked over to the bedroom door and opened it. "It's okay. I overreacted. I'm the one who should be sorry."

"Maddie?"

"Yes?"

"You know you should call Jorge."

"Here, catch," I said, and tossed the tape measure back to Gabriela. "The room is all yours."

Gabriela caught the tape measure and closed her hand around it. "Maddie. You really should call Jorge."

"I'm done trying, Gabby."

"He's changed, Maddie. I talked to him last night and he told me he's been volunteering with the Conservation Core, cleaning brush and mountain trails. And he's taking some other classes too."

"Conservation Core? I didn't know that."

"He's helping out with the wildfires."

"Jordan? Jordan is doing that?"

"Yes, *Jorge*," Gabriela said his name in Spanish, not the with a hard-edged "J" but a soft "H" and a rolling "R."

The name is soft, like colored chalk.

Horrr-hey.

CHAPTER 21

AFTER THE BARBECUE, AIDEN AND I DROVE UP Laurel Canyon. When we almost reached the top, at Mulholland Drive, the road snaked around left and right, and the air was suddenly thick with patches of fog.

I recounted my run-in with Gabriela. "I think I'm a bad sister."

Aiden reached over to take my hand. His thumb gently rolled over each of my fingertips, one by one. "No you're not. Not by a long shot. You have no idea," he said quietly. "If you want to talk about bad . . ." He paused. "I had a brother . . . once."

"Had? You've never said anything about a brother."

"I don't talk about him much. He was younger than me. His name was Alex," he said, almost in a whisper and I could barely make out the name.

"Alex? I saw his name in your book."

"It was his book. He had an accident . . . it was awhile back."

Behind us, the Valley was shimmering with lights.

Ahead, the road curved suddenly and Aiden took the turn too fast. His tires squealed.

"Slow down," I gulped, trembling from the sound of the tires.

"Sorry. Sorry about that."

"And Alex?" I asked, when my heart stopped pounding.

"He died."

I wanted to ask him more, when it had happened and how, but Aiden bit down hard on his bottom lip, and his eyes narrowed, focusing on the road. "I'm sorry. It's still hard for me to talk about it. Maybe another time."

"It's okay. We don't have to talk about it now."

He was quiet as he followed Laurel Canyon down into the city, then headed east toward Hollywood.

"I still think I could pass my birthparents on the street," I said, trying to revisit our conversation of the other day. "It could happen, you know. I could walk right past them on Central Park West or Broadway and not even know it."

"I don't think the very remote chance of seeing them is the real reason you're afraid to go to New York," he said, his eyes turning kelp green.

"I know." He was right, but that was okay. I liked the warm night and being alone with him. There was nothing in our way, and I wanted him to know. "It's just that math comes easy to me and always has. I think it's art, my collages, that I'm afraid of. They come too hard." They floated around in my head for weeks, treacherous with choices, unrelated objects and images that begged for connection. "I haven't put one piece together in weeks."

"I know. So why do we end up loving the things that come hardest?"

Every minute or so, bluish headlights came around the corner to light up Aiden's eyes and they were now ocean-blue.

"It's really sort of eerie, you know," Aiden continued. "I think there's one chapter that's the key to the story, kind of like an establishing shot. It's when the narrator meets up with this crazy beggar. He warns about signing on with Captain Ahab and he's the one who says that one signature can change a person's entire life. He's called . . ."

"The Prophet," I interrupted. "You're not really going to make your decision based on what that book says or doesn't say, are you?" I took a breath. "Because there's a big problem with *Moby Dick.*"

"What do you mean a big problem?"

"There isn't one woman character. And if a woman is alluded to at all, she's far off somewhere, waiting on land, as if she only belongs in some man's dream world."

"Oh, so you've actually been reading *Moby Dick?*" he said, pleased.

"Just skimming through."

"But I don't see the 'big' problem."

"There's no counterbalance to the story, no male and female. It's like a lopsided equation. But you know what? Never mind. I don't care what that book says."

"Why does everything have to be so complicated?"

"What else is complicated?"

"This morning I heard I might get an offer to work production on a feature film with a great director. This could be my once-in-a-lifetime chance, and I don't want to make the wrong decision."

"That's crazy timing."

"You know, maybe it was the same for your birthparents. Did you ever think it might have been a crossroads for them, some important opportunity or life's work, something they couldn't give up and that's why they gave you up?"

"Are you talking about my birthparents, about Olivia, or about yourself? In my case, I'm sure it didn't have anything to do with some great opportunity. If that was true, I could have lived with that. It was just a matter of hard numbers."

"Numbers?"

Sunset Boulevard was backed up, noisy with club goers, and we were barely inching forward. "Yes, numbers." And I repeated the theory I'd told Jorge.

"Numbers, that's crazy. That can't be it," Aiden said, but I could tell that my theory did get to him. "And by the way, there *is* a female character in the book. She's there from start to finish."

"That's impossible." I went over the book in my head. Had I missed something or someone in the book?

"It's the *Pequod*, the ship. Ships are always female. The ship is the counterbalance to the story," he said then became quiet. We were at a complete stop. "I want to tell you something, Maddie," he said softly, wrapping his arms around me.

Close, I could feel the heat coming off his skin. I rested my head on his shoulder. "I've been thinking about this a lot," he whispered, and his lips touched my cheek then the hollow beneath my ear. "And I want to tell you now, but this isn't the right place, not in a car, and not in the middle of bumper-to-bumper traffic."

I closed my eyes.

Everything was right, the night, his lips on my cheek. I didn't need to go anywhere else. I didn't need a better backdrop, but Aiden did, and a half hour later we were in the heart of Hollywood. Just off the Cahuenga exit on the freeway, the Capitol Records building sat on a hill like a stack of old records, its needle poking a hole into the skyline.

"I read that the light on the spire still flashes 'Hollywood' in Morse code," Aiden said, turning into a street called Ivar. It looked like an old 1920s neighborhood that had been sliced in half by the freeway. "This is where Nathanial West wrote *The Day of the Locust*. And up there," Aiden pointed to a spot higher up on the street, "are the Alto Nido apartments where they filmed a scene from *Sunset Boulevard*.

We got out of the car, and he took my hand in his. His palm was cool in the hot, damp night. The freeway hummed close by, and the small quiet street was dark and comfortable, like an old T-shirt. I reached down to pick up a penny I saw below the curb.

He turned to me. "We're going to run up this hill, together, then back down and fast."

I looked to the street. It was steep, the pavement uneven and broken with tree roots in parts. We could easily trip.

"You're kidding, right?"

"No, I'm perfectly serious. Trust me. You can do it. There's something about climbing up and then coming down, and the steeper the better. It's great for stirring up the creative juices. Trust me?"

"Is this another attempt to dislodge my creative block?"

"Maybe," he smiled. "Come on."

"Okay. I trust you."

Running straight up the street was hard, but the run down was even harder. My knees were shaking. I was fighting gravity the entire way, and my feet had a hard time keeping up with the momentum of the rest of my body. My instinct was to stiffen up and resist, my arms glued tight to my torso, and I was sure I was going into a freefall.

"Let go of your arms," Aiden said, smiling. "Bring them up," he exhaled. "Forty-five degree angle, palms up," he said, running beside me. I raised my arms, and they were my parachutes, slowing me down.

"Feels great, doesn't it?" he said, when we reached the bottom.

"Yesss," I barely managed to say, breathless and giddy at the same time. I took a deep breath. "Let's do it again."

The second time around, my knees were still shaking, and I was a little woozy, but it didn't frighten me. When we reached the bottom again he looked at me and lifted me off the ground.

"I've been thinking about things a lot," he started. "And I think I'm falling in love with you, and . . . I think you shouldn't be afraid of going to New York," he whispered.

He kissed the palms of my hands. And his words, the color of his kisses, and the dark night swallowed me up.

It's a color that has no name.

"I think I'm falling in love with you too."

CHAPTER 22

A FEW DAYS LATER, THE WEEKLY STAFF MEETING in the stockroom ran more than an hour late. The store's management had brought in some people from the corporate office to give us a thirty-minute animated PowerPoint presentation on the Ban the Plastic Grocery Bag protesters who had been picketing our store on and off for the last month. The first slide flashed across the screen like a spinning ball.

Convenience for Our Customers and Lost Jobs!

There was more—photos of unruly demonstrators and statistics in favor of single-use bags. I looked at my watch and fidgeted in my seat. The stock boy sitting next to me rolled his eyes and whispered, "What's the big deal about plastic bags?"

"I don't know," I shrugged, and looked at my watch again.

It was past ten p.m. when Aiden picked me up. We were heading to Twains again for something to eat, when we both spotted the lights at the same time. It was the

Sepulveda Dam, usually dark at that time of the night, but it was completely lit up, as if it were daylight.

Aiden slowed down. "We have to stop," he said then turned to me. "I hope you've got your camera with you."

"I do. But why?"

"It's a film shoot, and you're going to get the most unbelievable shots, I promise you."

There was no place to park, so Aiden had to drive about a quarter of a mile away to find parking. We backtracked to the dam by foot, walking over a freeway overpass. There were no pedestrians on the overpass at night, and it was pitch dark, except for the stream of car headlights, and I held on tight to Aiden's hand.

We crossed a freeway exit ramp then turned left onto a dirt path, following the yellow signs with black arrows, which pointed the way to crew parking and the film base camp. I'd been on the same path in the daytime but never at night, and everything was murky, my eyes having a hard time adjusting to the dark. It was a rare, muggy night, almost tropical, the humidity unsettling.

"This is a little creepy."

"Don't worry," he said. "You'll see."

The chain-link gate looked closed and padlocked, but when we got closer I could see there was a small opening, and we maneuvered our way through it then headed toward the lights. Lit up, the dam looked more like a castle fortress against a black sky. There was a large film crew with an encampment of tents and film trucks along with tables of food and racks of costumes. Nearby were the booms and lighting stands, cranes, jibs, and large screens.

"We're probably trespassing."

"Probably," he laughed.

We edged closer, and I could hear the sound of the generators, but we could also see there were people with flashlights patrolling farther ahead of us, and we stopped.

"I think this is close enough," I said, and I took out my camera.

Aiden had been right. The scene looked other-worldly, and everything seemed to be in movement. There were lights bouncing off screens and light stands against the dark sky and cars, blurred in motion as they raced under the shadow of the dam. Only the larger movie cameras sat still on giant tripods, like statues. I took my first shot, but didn't realize my camera was set on automatic, and the flash went off accidentally. I quickly turned it off and set the camera on manual.

"Lucky you. Security people didn't seem to notice," Aiden whispered.

I had taken some more photos when we suddenly heard someone talking into a bullhorn then saw a stunt-man climbing up the dam. When he reached the top, the man with the bullhorn shouted out instructions again. The stuntman took just a few running steps then leapt into the air, tucking himself into a ball. In a second he'd shot his legs out, and landed flat on a stack of mats laid out below him on the dry lakebed.

Twenty minutes later he repeated the same stunt. I was too far away for a good shot of him, and I didn't have a long-zoom lens. We crept closer, keeping an eye out for the flashlights, still far enough from us that they looked like dots of light in and out of the surrounding brush.

The man repeated the stunt again and again, and I kept shooting.

"I'm not sure I'm getting anything good," I whispered to Aiden.

"It's okay," he said. "To do something right, you have to be okay with failing."

I continued to shoot, but when I saw beams of flashlights, closer now, I grabbed Aiden's hand and started to run. I turned to look back and saw the beams crisscross each other, and we picked up the pace, sprinting back.

In the car, my palms were slick and I was breathing hard, but I had to look at the photos I'd taken right away, more than a hundred, I figured. I pressed the picture review button, and the images slid sideways across my screen. Aiden leaned in close, so he could see too.

"Dull. Dull. Too dark. Overexposed. Nothing special. Out of focus. Terrible." I moaned after each image. Halfway through, I stopped.

"Don't stop now. Keep going."

"Nothing. Nothing. Nothing," I continued. But then,

almost at the end, there was one. One shot of the stunt-
man suspended in the air, his arms and legs outstretched,
the dam just softly out of focus, and the bright lights like
a halo behind him. I passed the camera to Aiden.

"Just one out of a hundred," I said. "Not a great ratio."

"Not true. It's all you need, just one, just one perfect
shot," he said as he gave me back my camera and turned
on the engine.

CHAPTER 23

AIDEN CALLED IN THE MORNING TO TELL ME that Olivia and the baby had left for Canada.

"Are you okay?" I asked. He said he was, but he sounded down. "I have the day off. Let's do something offbeat?"

"Like what?"

I racked my brains for something, anything that might cheer him up. "How about we play tourists?" I proposed "A Hollywood bus tour? I heard there's a 'classic movie location tour.'"

Aiden liked the idea, but after I bought the tickets at a booth on Hollywood Boulevard, I was second-guessing myself. "Kind of a tame excursion compared to last night, right?" and I stopped on the first step of the mini-bus just as we were about to board. "Be honest. You can tell me if this is completely lame."

"No, this could be fun," Aiden said. "I bet there are a lot of little factoids I don't know. Good choice." And I was glad I'd nixed the lipstick-red, double-decker, bus of the usual sights and had opted for the more private "classic movie location" tour.

I settled down into the window seat of the twelve-seat minibus, only three-quarters full. Behind us I overheard someone talking about a deadly typhoon that had hit Taiwan, burying villages and trapping people. One hundred inches of rain had fallen in a short period, along with eighty-five-mile-per-hour winds, someone said, and I tried to imagine the torrent of water, streets that had become waterways. But one hundred inches of rain seemed impossible to visualize in the cool, dry, cocoon of the minibus.

While Aiden poured over the tour foldout, my brain zigzagged to the other night, the moment when Aiden had said he was falling in love with me. I remembered every little thing about it, the night, the sound of the freeway, but it was driving me crazy. I couldn't attach a number to how long it had lasted. Was it only one quick second? Thirty?

I reached into my jeans pocket for the penny I'd found that night, but my fingers landed on the slap tag I'd forgotten to throw away. I turned to the window, took it out and flipped it over. It was creased, but the sticky backing was intact, unused, and I quickly jammed it back into my pocket before Aiden noticed.

I turned to Aiden. He looked exhausted. "You okay?"

"I'm fine," he said, but I dug into the small cooler I'd brought along and handed him a bottled water. I took out a lemonade and peanut butter cookie for myself and scarfed them both down.

The tour started out at the Las Palmas Hotel, just

off Hollywood Boulevard, where Richard Gere had climbed up a fire escape for Julia Roberts in *Pretty Woman*, the guide pointed out, then to the Crossroads of the World, originally a shopping mall on Sunset Boulevard with a central building designed to resemble an ocean liner. It was surrounded by a small village of cottage-style bungalows, and was built in 1936. At each stop, a small DVD player at the front of the minbus screened a clip of the movie location we were visiting.

Aiden looked happy for awhile chatting with the tour guide, adding his own bits of movie trivia to the guide's presentation, as well as mixing it up with an older Texan couple, one row ahead of us, who couldn't seem to get enough of Aiden's jokes.

"The truth is, the baby would probably be better off without me," Aiden suddenly whispered in my ear, and the peanut butter cookie and lemonade sank to the bottom of my stomach. "I'm not sure I'm really fit to be a father," he confessed. "Besides, the job offer I told you about . . . it's in New York, and there's no way I can take an infant with me there."

New York.

My mind started to race imagining it, the two of us in New York, in slow-mo, like a corny chick flick scene. I saw myself with Aiden, a faraway camera zooming in on us on a crowded street, but the slow-mo froze.

"But why isn't there a way? There are plenty of single fathers in New York. They manage."

"I just don't know."

"So that's it? You've decided to give up the baby?" I was sick at the thought. The slow motion scene in my head switched to fast-forward and everything became a blur, like an action movie trailer photomontage, cut and pasted together in rapid-fire succession.

"No, not yet. I just needed to say it out loud," he admitted. "You know, to see how the words feel."

"Those words don't feel good," I said, and my head was getting heavier.

At the bottom of my pocket, I felt Jordan's old slap tag smoldering, burning to get out, and I dug down inside, feeling its edges. My stomach lurched.

We'd reached The Cat and the Fiddle, a British pub where some interior scenes from *Casablanca* were shot. The movie clip was iconic, a black and white fog surrounded Bergman and Bogart, Bogart's raincoat collar up as a fog rolled in, the two lovers reaching for each other in profile. I could feel the tension between them as they were about to part, two lone figures on a landing strip, the sound of an airplane engine in the background. The tour guide droned on about the location, with tidbits about Ingrid Bergman and Humphrey Bogart, when Aiden leaned in and whispered again.

"I don't know what to do."

"I know this isn't simple for you, I said.

His phone interrupted.

Aiden spoke low, but the tour guide called out to me.

"Hey, *chica*. Tell your boyfriend to get off the phone. No cell phones in here."

"*Chica*? Really?"

I felt a strange fury rise up inside me, and it radiated down to my hands. I reached deep into my pocket and took out Jordan's tag. Under the seat, I slowly separated the sticky part from its backing. The backing fell like a feather down to the mini-van floor, without a sound. But when I smacked the tag itself up on the back of the seat of the Texan couple in front of us, their seat bounced up just as Aiden put down his phone.

"You," the tour guide called out again from the back of the bus. "What do you think you're doing there?"

I froze, unable to move or speak. Everybody on the bus was looking directly at me.

"I'm talking to you, *chica*," the guide yelled out again, and marched angrily toward me.

Aiden shot me a quick fierce look, but stood up and planted himself between the guide and me. "No worries, man, we're leaving," Aiden said, putting both hands up and further blocking the guide's way.

"Not before your little friend here scrapes that crap off the seat."

"Seriously, man. It's not a big deal. There's no damage. See . . . here, I'm taking it off right now," Aiden said, and in a second he kneeled down and peeled off the slap tag.

"I still think I should call the police."

I looked at Aiden, but my feet were stapled to the floor.

"Really, no need for that, man," Aiden stood up again and calmly reassured the guide.

"All right, just get out of here," the guide continued. "And don't even think about ever coming back on one of my tours."

"We're going," Aiden said, pulling me up and out of the seat and out the front door of the bus.

They left us on the hot sidewalk. Cars rushed past on Sunset Boulevard and Aiden mumbled something about how were we going to get back to his car, parked four miles away.

"What's the matter with you, Maddie?" Looking down at his hand, he noticed he was still holding the slap tag, and crushing it, he threw it down on the pavement. "What does it mean to you?"

"What does what mean?" My head was a hurricane of half thoughts, and I struggled to understand him.

"That infinity sign on the tag."

"I . . . I . . ." I couldn't finish my sentence.

"What does it mean?" Aiden insisted.

"It means . . . it means—"

"What does it mean to you? And why? Why do you have it?"

In math, infinity was sometimes treated as if it were any other number. Its symbol, the rotated eight, was a perfect representation of something without limit, without end. "I used to scribble it on all my school notebooks, then Jordan saw it, and did the same. But then

Jordan used it—for his gang sign. I wish I'd never done it."

Aiden gently took hold of me by both shoulders. "Are you okay?"

"I'm sorry, I'm so sorry," I stuttered, looking down at the sidewalk, cracked in a hundred places.

"What were you thinking?"

I thought of Jordan. But I couldn't blame him for this. "I don't know." I was trembling, my face streaked with tears. "I really don't know."

I wasn't even very clear about it, remembering only bits and pieces of what had happened. I only remembered the way my hand felt heavy beneath the seat, but then how easily I'd pushed the feather-light tag upward. Was that how Jordan felt when he'd roamed the dark streets at night, both heavy and weightless at the same time?

There was a buzzing in my ears, and I tried to focus on something, anything. I saw the black wrought iron wrapped around the balconies and windows of the restaurant. They were intricate, filigreed and curling, but it was as though I'd been thrown into Miles's old parabolic flight simulator at Boeing, zero gravity unleashed, and my knees started to buckle. Aiden wrapped his arms around me and gently propped me up. He bought me a drink and we sat on a bus bench until I felt better, and then we slowly walked the four miles back to the car.

That night I couldn't fall asleep, and I walked down the hall to Jordan's old room. The door was closed. Only

Leah went in once a week to vacuum. I opened the door and turned on the light. There were Jordan's old school books piled up in one corner, his video game cassettes still on his desk, and it looked like nothing had been moved or touched. I looked up at the ceiling. When I was twelve, I'd helped Jordan paint the ceiling midnight-blue, then we both stood on his bed, jumping up to stick on glow-in-the-dark stars. By the time I was thirteen, though, he'd ripped off all the stars, and the ceiling became pitch black.

I turned off the light and laid down on Jordan's floor. Looking up, I saw the one glow-in-the-dark star that Jordan had missed. It still emitted a tiny, luminescent green, and I curled up as tight as I could into a ball and fell asleep beneath it.

January 11, 2008

Dear Alex—

It's 7:00 p.m. The sea is lurching, angry, and brutal beneath the inflatable boat, and I fight hard to keep my bearings and my balance. We use a water spray to frustrate the harpooner's aim, but they also use larger water cannons on us, and the water itself, its abundance, becomes a weapon against them and against us. Despite all our planning and training, I feel like we're scrambling.

Water is everywhere and my eyes are blurry with the torrent. There's a furious wind and my hands are shaking, but I try to record what my eyes see through the lens. The small inflatable boat zigzags in front of the path of the whaling ship at a dizzying speed, but the hunter ship almost rams into us. "Too close, too close," someone yells above the din of the water and their foghorn.

We veer away from the ship.

Close. The word runs through me. Did I ever tell you what Mom said to me after you were born? She told me she wanted your name to begin with an "A" because she wanted the two of us to be close to one another, Aiden and Alex, like twins, even though we were more than three years apart. "It's what every mother wants," she said, "for her children to be close." I have never felt closer to you than now.

We turn around and aim for the ship again.

I know the hunter ship is bigger than the Esperanza, but from the tiny inflatable it's even more enormous, and our smallness is frightening. Men in yellow helmets on the upper decks of the hunter ship look down at us from above, lining the decks. Maybe I'm hallucinating, but they look like chessmen to me. They yell down and mock us. They throw rocks and rotten food and chains at us. We've become their prey, but that's exactly what we're here to do. No matter what, we're prepared to stand our ground.

My heart is beating so fast, and I'm sweating, even in this cold. All along I thought I was doing this for you, but now I understand I was wrong.

You brought me here.

You brought me here to do this for myself.

Al – ways –
Aiden

CHAPTER 24

THE ALARM NEAR MY BED RANG LOUDLY.

I grabbed the fire extinguisher training manual I should have studied last night, but hadn't. I started reading for today's training, but the words and diagrams kept moving around on the page.

I focused on the blaze-red photo of an extinguisher and flattened down the page of the manual. I started again.

There were three types of fires, A-types, which were common combustible, such as wood, paper, cloth; and then there were B-types, flammable liquids, such as gas, oil and grease. Then there were C-types, electrically energized fires, started by computers, toasters and heaters. But there were four kinds of fire extinguishers, water, dry chemical, carbon dioxide and halon.

I went over it once more—the water extinguisher shouldn't be used on electrical or flammable liquid fires. The carbon dioxide extinguisher could only be used for flammable liquids and electrical fires, but you couldn't hold the cone-shaped nozzle because it might freeze your hand.

My head was reeling with instructions and facts by the time I reached the old fire station in the heart of Van Nuys. I looked up at the Deco-era entrance. "Engine Company No. 39" was etched deep above the three garage doors.

First, we practiced what to do when someone's clothing was on fire, employing the stop, drop, and roll technique. We took turns covering our eyes, dropping to the ground, and rolling back and forth until the fire was robbed of all its oxygen.

Then a firefighter demonstrated an upholstery fire, lighting a match and dropping it on a sofa. The materials used for sofas and chairs allowed fires to penetrate more deeply and smolder inside for a long time, the firefighter said.

Next was PASS—Pull the pin, Aim at the base of the fire, Squeeze the handle, Sweep the fire, I repeated to myself, as each team member took a turn using the fire extinguisher.

In the first five minutes, a small fire could heat up the ceiling of a room to over a thousand degrees, the instructor told us. Then materials break down, releasing vapors that spread across the room in one rapid sweep. A flashover of a room could happen in less than two minutes.

It was my turn now. They prepared a small electrical fire in a pit, and I had to quickly choose the correct extinguisher, but I hesitated. I wasn't sure which one.

It's the one in the middle, I thought I heard someone

say behind me. It sounded like Jordan, but when I turned around, there was no one there.

I pull the pin, and the air turns dust-gray, and it's okay; the fire is out.

CHAPTER 25

TWO DAYS LATER, AIDEN PICKED ME UP TO GO out for lunch, but first, he said, he needed to drop off some paperwork.

"About what happened," I began. "About that slap tag . . ."

"Let's just forget it."

"But I want to . . ."

"No really, Maddie. It's not a big deal," he said, in a straightforward tone of voice, and without even a trace of irritation. "You made a mistake, and I get that. Believe me, I've made plenty of my own."

"But don't you think we should talk about it?"

"It's okay. No use talking. It's done."

I should have been relieved, but I wasn't.

I hadn't been paying much attention to where we were going until I realized we were near the Van Nuys civic center. Sitting mid-valley, the governmental center housed the Van Nuys city hall, a library, police station, and two county courthouses. A string of storefront law offices and bail bondsmen dotted the boulevard. I began to fidget in my seat when Aiden found a parking space at a meter in back of the city hall. It was across from the same fire station where I'd taken the fire extinguisher training.

"A sign?" I muttered under my breath.

Aiden looked at me. "Now it's you looking for signs?" Aiden turned to grab a small stack of papers from the back seat and put them on his lap. "I was wrong. There are no signs, and there are no answers in *Moby Dick*," he suddenly announced, completely miserable. "No methodology to figure out my life."

"Don't say that."

Aiden picked up the papers from his lap. "I'll be right back," he said, as he swung the car door open, I wondered whether the papers were adoption forms, but I was afraid to ask and watched him walk away.

He looked crushed, like Jordan had looked back then, at the end of our last trip to the desert. Miles had taken us to the high desert to see the double Leonid meteor showers. Jordan had carped about coming along but when we set up the lawn chairs to watch, he reached over to take my hand. I heard him suck in his breath when we saw the trails of light marking the sky. Miles told us about the Tempel-Tuttle comet, lecturing us about the speed it traveled and the grazers that didn't drop down into the earth's atmosphere, but fell outside the Earth's surface. I imagined the clouds of particles, the meteors burning up as they entered the atmosphere. Then Jordan presented his theory to Miles.

Part budding scientist, part philosopher, Jordan was already starting to butt heads with Miles. He'd had lots of theories about luck, destiny, and coincidence, his latest hypothesis being the theory that the generation of simultaneous positive thoughts from a controlled number of people could trigger a positive shift in humanity. But Miles glossed over Jordan's theory, telling him it was a nice thought, but impossible to prove—"a naïve hypothesis," he called it. It was at that moment that I could see it, the light that went out of Jordan's eyes, and the entire way home Jordan didn't say a word.

The Van Nuys city hall looked like a copy of the larger, Los Angeles city hall in downtown, also a Deco structure with a base of buildings shaped like an *H* and a central tower. I looked up to see the beautiful cream-on-terra cotta colored friezes.

But across the street, the fire station doors lifted open and two fire trucks bolted out, leaving piercing sirens in their wake. I held my hands up to my ears. Alone in the car, I imagined Aiden handing an adoption form across a counter, then an inky red date stamp pressed coldly into the fabric of the paper. I could almost hear the sound of it smacking down on the counter, and I flung the car door open.

People bustled past me on the sidewalk and I dug out my camera, pointing it to the steps. I took one shot, then another in exactly the same position, ten seconds later, continuing to take a shot every ten seconds for five minutes, thirty shots in all. Stitching them together would create a stop motion clip, people magically appearing and disappearing from one frame to another, like shooting stars.

I sat back down in the car and scrolled through the photos, again and again. The steps filled up with people, then suddenly became empty, full, then empty, stopping time, when Aiden appeared at the car door.

"Done."

"What's done?"

"Location permits for my boss. I wasn't too long was I?"

I breathed a sigh of relief. "No, not at all."

"Now that that's done, what are you doing later tonight?" Aiden asked. "I saw that there's a Truffaut film at the Nuart in the city," he said. "I think they're playing *Jules and Jim*."

"Yes," I said. I reached out for Aiden's hand, and I could feel each one of the small bones of his fingers. "Sure."

CHAPTER 26

AFTER LUNCH WITH AIDEN, I WENT TO THE NEXT CERT class. The grainy, cell-phone video clip they showed us was short, barely a minute. It was an example of a landslide that had knocked a house off of its foundation a year ago, just north of Los Angeles. But mudslides didn't always occur because of heavy rain, our trainer told us. Groundwater flowing through cracked bedrock could trigger a movement of soil and slopes that had been altered for construction of roads or houses were at risk.

He replayed the clip.

This time, I could see that the ground above the house was barren and the slide started off slow, just a trickle of rocks and dirt until it gathered up momentum. It came down with a rumble of uprooted trees and rocks, snapping electrical wires, sending the entire hillside crashing onto the roof of a house below in just seconds. At the end of the clip, we heard the cell phone user yell and saw the scene turn sideways when his phone dropped on the ground and he scrambled for safety.

Look for tilted trees and telephone polls.

Listen for rumbling sounds.

Move to higher ground.

Next, we moved outside for a lesson in sandbagging. I'd thought sandbags acted as a dam, but I was wrong. It was a way to divert debris flow down a better path, the trainer emphasized, then he distributed shovels, gloves, and sandbags.

We split up into three-person teams, each team with fifty sandbags to fill. One person shoveled, while another held the bag open, and a third transported the bag to a pallet. I started off with the shovel, making sure it was only a half load each time, so as to not spill the sand. Then I switched off with my team member, holding up the bag of sand. By the fortieth sandbag, my arms and back were aching badly. I asked to switch again, this time, passing the sandbags down. We were in two lines, spaced out so we could pass the bag forward to one another.

I was at the end of the line and made sure each sandbag overlapped the previous one, stamping them firmly into place.

CHAPTER 27

I CAME HOME FROM THE CLASS, WENT UPSTAIRS TO my room and took a long nap. Later, Aiden called to apologize and say that he wouldn't be able to make it to the Truffaut film. His supervisor had called, last minute, and had asked him to work on location again, this time on a night shoot, and he couldn't say no.

My arms were still a little achy from the sandbags when I came down the stairs to find Leah sitting on the living room floor, surrounded by boxes. She'd been on a new decluttering tear, throwing and giving things away, and had already tackled the hall closet a few days ago, pulling out decades-old stuff. Now she was attacking the dusty piles of stuff that had accumulated on both sides of the fireplace.

"Where's Dad?"

"Out, at a business meeting."

"You're still organizing, I see."

She looked up at me. "This place needs some refreshing," she said. "And by the way, Maddie, I put buckets in all the showers. We can use the runoff grey-water to water the outdoor plants."

"What's next, Mom?" I laughed. "Communal showers?"

Miles had already installed faucet and shower aerators and low-flow toilets, along with the little Post-It reminders he put up in all the bathrooms about three-minute showers and no running the water when brushing teeth.

"Time to make changes around here, recalibrate the numbers."

"Now you're really talking like Dad," I laughed again, but the phrase stuck in my head and with a little time now on my hands, I decided to drive over to Miles's mailbox store. I hadn't crunched the numbers for him in months and I took the canyon road over to Beverly Hills, past a 1960s-era gas station that had once been Jordan's favorite place. Jordan was twelve when he'd first spotted the gas station, begging Miles to stop and get gas under the long, fluorescent lights, glowing like the sleek underbelly of a spaceship. As Miles pumped the gas, Jordan would look up and mimic the sound of a rocket ship, and I would feel it too, the distinct possibility that if we closed our eyes, the two of us might just blast off into space.

It was late when I unlocked the back door, and it was stuffy in the storeroom where Miles kept his desk and computer along with the accounts receivable and next day bills, all of which were stacked and ready for payment. On one side of the backroom there were boxes taped up for packing, their labels affixed for shipping the next day.

I turned on the air and took down Miles's ledger books from the shelf above the desk. I opened the door into the main store. There were three large copiers on one side, paper, bubble wrap, and mailing tubes on another. The wall of gold mailboxes was in perfect order. The smaller mailboxes on top, each one with its own keyhole, numbers climbing in single digits from left to right. Then there were the larger boxes in the last two rows above the floor. But when I looked up, I saw the dried-out water stains on the drop ceiling above and the Christmas ornaments hanging from the metal ceiling frame that should have been taken down months ago.

I then got the mail, separating it into piles, and distributed each person's letters into the right box. Number 14 had the most mail. He was an old customer of Miles's, a retired professor who received a ton of academic journals every month. Number 101 was mostly into muscle and body building magazines, but Number 307 was the most interesting, a woman who received a single handwritten letter and nothing else once a month. I looked closely at the envelope. It was made from paper thick with texture. It didn't have a return address but had a foreign stamp, and Miles always joked that the woman probably had a secret lover stashed away in Europe. Curious, I held it up to the light, but it was opaque and I couldn't see through it.

Afterward, I logged on to Miles's accounting program, going through all the numbers once and then again. The numbers didn't add up, so I backtracked over the hardcopies of the books, this time all the way back into the last nine months. But no matter how many times I went over them, the numbers were clear. Miles was losing money, lots of money. There was no doubt the store was going under, and there was no way Miles could possibly afford to pay for tuition and housing at a private art school on the other side of the country.

I thought about Box Number 307's letter, the handwriting curling up into sly loops, and I knew. There were other secrets hidden away in Miles's office.

I looked down at his desk and began pulling out all the drawers. The top drawer was filled with old, four-year-old purchase orders and invoices. Below that, the middle drawer was bulging with the same, only older. Finally, the last drawer was an untidy heap of papers.

But under the bottom of the last drawer sat a thin, paper box on the floor. I opened it. Inside, there were three files, each with a name on the top right hand corner in thick, black Magic Marker, "Jordan", "Maddie," and "Gabriela." They were the originals of all the adoption papers and birth certificates. I'd seen a copy of mine long ago, but never Jordan and Gabriela's. I read over my own papers first, then Jordan's, and then Gabriela's, and my heart stopped.

I'd always thought it was just a coincidence that both

Jordan and Gabriela's mothers were named Maria. But reading carefully, I realized the fathers' names were the same too.

Blood pounded in my eyes, and the room began to spin. It all added up. Gabriela and Jordan had always had some special bond. I read over the papers one more time, comparing addresses and their birthparents' birthdates, but there was no doubt.

Gabriela and Jordan were true brother and sister.

I was the only odd person out.

I felt sick, and I bent over in the chair, putting my head down between my knees. I didn't know how long I sat there at Miles's desk like that, just trying to breathe. It seemed as though I was there for a long time, unable to move.

Suddenly, I remembered them together, Gabriela and Jordan, how they'd stuck together like glue the entire trip, that horrible trip down to Guatemala.

The colonial city of Antigua had been draped in bougainvillea, the extinct Aqua Volcano rising like a whisper above the city, but I couldn't find anything I liked about it. The incessant heat and humidity were suffocating; even the bushes full of flowers near the hotel seemed dark, robbing me of air. Trying to cheer me up, Leah gave me a camera she'd bought especially for me for the trip.

"Maybe you'll see things differently through a camera," she'd said.

"Don't think so," I'd frowned, but I was curious.

A week later, we'd traveled to the area of Tikal Peten in the northern part of the country. The trees were huge and the tour guide said the area was called the "lungs of the planet." Seeing the trees rush by me from the road, I could suddenly breathe again, and I hung my head out the back window, gulping down mouthfuls of air.

When we reached the lost city of Tikal, Mayan pyramids stood towering over the jungle floor. We explored the mazes of passageways and stairs. The "place of echoes," Leah read out loud from her guidebook. "It's the hidden Rebel base," Jordan cried out, finding a branch and playing Luke Skywalker the rest of the afternoon.

I took out the camera Leah had given me and started with a few tentative shots of the temples, one called the Great Jaguar, another the Temple of the Snake. By the time I'd walked around the perimeters of the stone ruins, I'd gotten the hang of the camera and took some close-ups of the greenstone masks and wall glyphs. The city had once been the home of ancient astronomers and mathematicians, mirroring the stars, and on that day everything was full of light.

But darkness returned with a rainstorm. The rain pounded on our car as we made our way to the village of El Remate, at the rim of a lake, and my breathing became shallow. I knew where Leah and Miles were taking me: to Alma and Rafael's village.

"I never want to meet them. They gave me up," and I didn't get out of the car.

Night was falling slowly, and soft lights lit up the windows of Alma and Rafael's small house. My parents stood at the doorstep, and Jordan and Gabriela remained outside. The car window was still beaded with rain and I could only see colors through it and my own tears, the ochre walls and the blue of a fading sky. The colors washed over Jordan and Gabriela, painting them with the same brush.

Sometime later, I put the adoption papers back in the box and shoved it under the bottom drawer. I suddenly hated the mailbox store, all the brown boxes and their labels, every package of toner and office supplies, every paper clip and ream of business stationary. I looked at the boxes Miles had lined up for shipping the next day. They all had their *This Side Up* labels neatly attached, arrows pointing upward. Up or down, this side or that. It didn't matter. And I sat down on the floor and sobbed.

A—

*The whalers are yelling into their bullhorns from above us,
and our inflatable boat knocks like a ragdoll against the
bottom of their ship. But there's so much sound coming
from the bullhorns and the sea that the sounds converge
into an eerie racket of silence.*

*Then flashes of light and the loud pops of stun
grenades rain down on us.*

*The stun grenades do exactly what they're meant to
do. The flashes of light are blinding and I feel like I've
been punched in the face. My arms and legs move
somehow, but in slow motion, like an old movie.*

*There's a ringing in my ears, and I think I've gone
completely deaf.*

Aiden

CHAPTER 28

IT WAS AFTER MIDNIGHT WHEN I RETURNED HOME. THE house was dead quiet, and I was exhausted, but I couldn't fall asleep. Jordan and Gabby were biological siblings. Just one piece of paper had upended everything.

I sat up in my bed and turned the light on, reaching for the copy of *Moby Dick* I'd left, mostly unread, on my nightstand. Somehow, I had to read it all, and now. It took me a long time to get into it, the irregular chapters, the endless minutia of whaling, but then I found myself getting lost in the smaller stories and descriptions; faraway places, from Cape Horn to Nantucket; and characters like Queequeg the tattooed Polynesian harpooner, Fedallah the mysterious Persian fire worshipper, and Specksynder, Stubb, and Dough Boy. Mostly, though, I scoured the book for words and phrases, anything that might convince Aiden to keep his baby, sure that the book was the only way to dissuade him from giving up his daughter. But I found nothing, no meaningful words, and I was running out of time. I finally fell asleep, but the alarm woke me up before the sun appeared.

I had an early morning shift and I dressed quickly and carefully shut the front door, happy to leave the house before my parents were up. Leah had started watering the potted plants on the doorstep, and had bought a bright new welcome mat, but no new mat could blot out what I'd discovered in the store last night.

I looked up, and beyond the street was the blur of the mountains in the distance, and I felt the onset of the dry, Santa Ana winds making their way from the Mojave desert, but even with the wind kicking up a bit, the sun was already insistent.

Before I unlocked the door to my car, though, I heard the sound of a familiar engine. It was Miles's old VW Bug, puttering down the street, the sound of the car arriving long before it was visible.

The twenty-five-year-old car, mustard yellow and rusting, was showing its age. Dad looked worn out too.

"Where have you been so early?" I asked.

"I've been driving around," he sighed. "I met with my accountant last night, and . . . we have to talk," Miles said, opening the car door. He'd left the engine on, but the aging AC, barely cold, had no chance against the heat. He was sweating in his collared shirt and tie. He looked terrible, like the summer he'd gotten his pink slip, when he would lock himself up in his study for hours, searching for job leads, rewriting his resume over and over again.

"I had to tell you first . . . even before Mom . . . I

really don't think we can afford to send you there, to New York, to art school, Maddie. The business is in trouble. I'm going to have to sell it at a loss," he said, turning off the engine and getting out of the car.

"I know."

"You know?" He closed the car door and took refuge under the shade of a pine tree. It was the largest pine on the street, a mass of needles and conifers that tilted and stretched upward hundreds of feet.

"I looked over the books last night. Why didn't you tell me before?"

"You were at the store? Last night?" he asked.

"You can stop worrying. I've been leaning against going to New York anyway."

"You have?" he asked, looking both guilty and relieved.

"Yeah, I think I should stick to math. It's a known quantity, safe, right?" I tried to sound convincing. "But why didn't you tell me?"

"I didn't want you to worry."

"I'm not talking about that."

"Then what?" he asked, but from his expression I knew he'd guessed.

He reached over and took my face in his hands for a moment, then kissed me on my cheek.

"About Gabriela and Jordan."

"You found the papers?" he murmured.

Something moved near a neighbor's rose bushes, just

a small rustle. I turned to see it was a mangy coyote, his brownish tail hanging limply. Coyotes were rare sights in the flats, but the lack of water this summer had been bringing them down from the hills, deeper into the Valley. I'd been startled one night by a pack, scavenging for food, yellow-eyed. But this one looked scrawny and lost, alone in the harsh sunlight without his pack.

"Why didn't you tell me?"

"We didn't want you to think that it mattered. And it doesn't. It doesn't matter that Gabriela and Jorge are biological siblings."

"It does matter. It matters to me."

Miles moved out of the shade of the pine tree and the sun pressed hard on the top of his head. "I'm so sorry, Maddie. We were going to tell you."

I heard another rustle. The coyote was still there, but he didn't look lost now. More like he was watching over us.

Miles cleared his throat and took a minute to collect his thoughts. "Don't be mad at your mom. Parents make mistakes, Maddie. And I know we've made plenty of them. But we were only doing what we thought was right."

I looked to the rose bushes, but the coyote had vanished.

"Forgive me?" Miles asked, looking completely despondent, and I couldn't help it. I fell into my father's arms, his silly, buttoned-down engineer's shirt, felt white and cool against my temple.

The rest of the day leached slowly. My entire shift

was spent training on one of the new self-service check-out machines the supermarket had recently acquired and was testing out.

"Those kiosks are going to make all us cashiers extinct," my manager said, shaking his head. "Extinct like the dinosaurs."

By the end of the six-hour training session, my head was full of barcodes, beeps, and the flashes of the scanner light. Nearby, the automatic door opened and shut to the rhythm of the touch screen woman's saccharin voice reciting the prices, and how much the shopper had saved.

I couldn't wait to get out of there Aiden was waiting for me at Jack's house. I took off my apron and threw it my locker, then looked at my phone and noticed a missed call from Jordan, but I didn't call him back.

CHAPTER 29

I FOUND AIDEN IN JACK'S KITCHEN WITH A BUCKET, mopping the floor. He looked up at me and smiled. "Want to take a turn?" he asked and held out the mop as if it was a relay baton.

I gave him a funny look. "Really?"

"It's a good brain exercise," he said. "It kind of quiets your mind, you know. This was my first job on the ship," he laughed.

"So, is this yet another one of your attempts at clearing away my artistic roadblocks?"

"Maybe." He grinned.

I laughed and took the mop from him. "Next you'll be teaching me how to tie nautical knots?" I asked, giving the floor a couple of swipes.

"Maybe that, too. One day."

Afterward, Aiden showed me around Jack's house. Aiden's bedroom was at the end of a long, narrow hallway, an add-on room Jack had built. His bed was loosely made, but I could see the dip in the pillow where his head had lain. I'd been only half-right about the colors of his room. Not celadon or cerulean, but more like the heat of lapis.

Aiden told me Jack liked to cook, and the kitchen was warm, shiny copper pots and pans hanging from the ceiling above the stove. The one-car garage was crammed with old film equipment Jack had collected over the years, and a wall of framed photographs of actors along with their inscriptions to Jack. Back in the house, the three computer screens in the living room were still dark and empty, the speakers on both sides soundless.

Later, we sat on the living room couch that overlooked the street, Aiden at the corner, one arm hung over the armrest, his feet up on the coffee table. I was tucked between his other arm and his chest, and through the window I could see a Water and Power truck pull up to the fire hydrant across the street.

"Sorry about last night," he apologized again. "My supervisor was really happy with my work. He said he'd give me a good recommendation for the production job in New York."

My heart started to jump. "New York? Does that mean you're not . . ."

"It doesn't mean anything yet. Nothing's decided. Really, I promise."

Across the street, one of the Water and Power workers uncapped the valve on the side of the hydrant, then took out a large, long wrench, and slowly released the bolt on the top.

I sat up. "What are they doing out there?"

Aiden looked to where I was pointing. "I think they're checking on the water pressure," Aiden replied, and a strong jet of water rushed out of the valve, reaching clear across the street.

I asked him how the editing on his film was going. "Not very good. It's been months since I shot the footage and I haven't made any real headway."

I burrowed my head deeper into his chest. "It was a bad night for me." And I told him about the birth certificates I'd discovered in Miles's store.

He sat up. "I hate that. I hate secrets," he said. "People spend so much time trying to cover up their secrets, but they end up bleeding out anyway."

"I just want to forget about it for now." I didn't want to think about Miles or the store or birth certificates. Or secrets.

Still, there was my secret, the one I'd kept covered up these past months, the one I hadn't shared with anyone. And I knew it wanted to come out too, to be exposed, just like the slap tag I'd pulled out of my pocket in the minibus.

"I told you that first day that I'm the kind of person who likes to put everything out there in the open, and I am, mostly, but . . . I have a secret too," I paused then started again. "It was the day Jordan went AWOL from his placement and, along with his friends, ended up vandalizing the warehouse. I'd seen Jordan earlier that day. He seemed upset and angry about the placement, complaining about the people who were in charge. But I'd heard Jordan's complaints before, and I wasn't very sympathetic. It was the worst fight we ever had."

Aiden looked at me. "Siblings fight all the time, Maddie."

"But then I did something. I egged Jordan on. 'Why don't you just run away,' I told him, practically daring him to do it. And he did go AWOL. And it was my fault he wrecked his probation."

"That can't be true," Aiden said, holding me closer. "There has to be another explanation."

I got up from the couch, went to the kitchen, and poured a couple of iced teas from a pitcher in the fridge, bringing them, along with some sweetener packets, back to the coffee table.

"I've gone over it again and again, and it's the only conclusion I can come to."

"But did you ask your brother about it?"

"No, I couldn't."

I settled back into the couch with Aiden. He flicked a packet of sweetener back and forth between his thumb and forefinger. "I can't believe it," he said, tearing the packet in half.

"What's the matter?"

"Just my luck. Empty."

The tiny, torn packet landed in two pieces, flamingo-pink, on the floor. I picked up the pieces and examined them.

"You're right, it's empty."

"Not good," Aiden said, shaking his head. "Not a good sign. How many millions of these do they make?" And I could suddenly feel the Santa Ana winds now breathing in the canyons, the threat of firestorms and falling trees. Aiden was talking as though an empty Sweet 'N Low packet was a prophecy. "I'm a jinx. That's the real reason I shouldn't be a father."

"What do you mean a jinx?"

"It's my secret and my lie. My dad told me never to talk about it, but that's the problem with a secret, it wants to be told, right? And a secret is no better than a lie, a lie of omission."

"I don't understand."

"I told you about my brother, Alex, about his accident . . . I didn't tell you everything. I was there with him when it happened. We were together."

"You saw the accident?"

"No. Worse. I'm the reason for the accident."

"I don't understand."

"Alex was an unbelievable kid, so smart. He'd already skipped two grades and would stay up all night reading. He couldn't get enough of the classics. He spent his allowance buying up every paperback classic he could find at garage sales. And he loved going out on Jack's sailboat. There wasn't one weekend he didn't beg my parents to go out on the boat, never mind the weather.

"Even at twelve years old he was writing letters to

the president, collecting money to save the seals, then the dolphins, turtles, and whales." Aiden took another deep breath. "My parents were out for the day and I was supposed to keep an eye on him. I was fifteen and I wasn't exactly happy about babysitting. It was summer, just around the longest day of the year. It was eight o'clock, but there was still light outside, and Alex asked me to come outside with him to try out his new bike. I was playing some stupid video game and didn't want to stop, so he sneaked out without me. The hit and run driver blew past the stop sign and never even slowed down."

He didn't have to describe it for me to imagine it, the bicycle airborne, his brother on the ground, tire tracks on the street, the boy's face, bone to black asphalt, his cheek folded into his eye.

"Hit and run. That's horrible."

"You don't get it," he said, and he took little, shallow breaths, his voice almost inaudible. "I was supposed to take care of him. I should never have let him get out of my sight. I let everybody down," Aiden said, and his words burned with regret.

"But it wasn't your fault."

"You don't understand, Maddie. Alex is dead, and it was my fault."

"It was an accident, a terrible accident. You can't blame yourself."

"Everyone told me that, at the hospital, and then at Alex's funeral, but they were wrong."

"What do you mean 'wrong'?"

"Ever since it happened, it's like the universe keeps trying to tell me that I'm bad luck. Things just fall all around me. I swear, Maddie. First, it was just me. I'd be clumsy and drop things, the grocery bag, pens, paper. Things would just slip out of my hands. But then it got worse. I took a walk down my street and a bird fell out of its nest, landing right in front of me. I tried, but I couldn't save it, and I knew then I was a curse to everything and everyone around me. And I couldn't even go to visit my own brother's grave, Maddie. Not once. Then you . . ." and he stopped.

My heart was breaking for Aiden and I reached over and gathered him up in my arms. His head fell heavily against my chest. "But I don't understand."

"It was you who ended the curse. I stopped you and your friend from falling that day at the camera store," he said, almost sobbing. "You did that for me. We stopped it from happening, you and me together."

I looked across the street. The workers were replacing the valve cap and retightening the top bolt. I saw the montage in my head, Alex's accident, flurries of tiny feathers descending, pens dropping, and bags and glass broken on the sidewalk, and then, the water-soaked floor and Aiden gripping Bryn's hand. And I wanted to hold Aiden like that, for hours, for days, against my chest, to keep him safe.

January 12, 2008

Dear Alex—

The sounds merged then too. First, there was the sound of your heartbeat in the ICU, the other beeps of the monitors and machines, and the sucking in and out of the respirator. Then complete silence, and Mom on the floor, howling.

Later that night, after the hospital, we came home and they started shouting at each other. They were arguing about how to bury you and where to bury you. I couldn't blame them for not being prepared, for not understanding how to navigate the worst waters of their life, but I couldn't stand the sound of it. Dad wanted your body cremated, your ashes scattered at sea. Mom wanted a traditional funeral, where she could go and visit, she said, where she could bring flowers and sit and touch your gravestone. Dad said you'd devoted yourself to the ocean. Mom said she couldn't live with the thought of your life scattered to the winds. They went back and forth like that for two days until they finally agreed to a spot near a lake, on some property Jack's family had owned just north of Los Angeles, so you would hear the sound of water in your eternity.

It was the middle of summer and it shouldn't have rained, but it rained the day we put your ashes to rest. The rain kept coming and wouldn't let up. It was just like an old movie, black umbrellas ballooning up against a gray sky. It rained so hard I thought the lake would overflow. The service was short; only Dad and Jack spoke. I wanted to say something too, but I couldn't bear to hear my own voice.

Later, all their sadness and shock percolated into

anger and blame, but no one would say it. No one would blame me, and I wished they would. I hated the lie they told themselves. They blamed each other, and the hit and run driver, but never the real culprit: me.

Months later, the police came and told us the hit-and-run driver had been found and identified, and there was a month-long trial. There were diagrams and photos, expert witnesses that droned on about the position of your body, the marks on your bicycle and the car, and the angle of the sun at that hour, on that day. It almost killed Mom and Dad to relive it, to hear his excuses, and I sat in the courtroom and wished the police had never found the driver, because it was like you dying all over again.

More than a year went by, and then it happened. I felt my own anger rise up in me. I couldn't blame myself anymore, and I started to blame you. You knew better than to go out alone on your bike when the sun was setting, when the sun could blind you. You were smart and knew, too, that you shouldn't have gone out without me. I was angry that you left me alone to deal with Mom and Dad, and that I would have to be the one to make up for you, to be your stand-in for the rest of my life. I was mad that I would have to live your life and not my own. I was angry and bitter and broken.

The anger did ebb, slowly. With time, like the tide, it left and returned, and still returns to me sometimes. But here, on this ship, in the middle of this roiling, bedlam of ocean and ship, and bullhorns, the anger finds me once again.

Al - ways -
Aiden

CHAPTER 30

THE IMAGE CAME TO ME IN THE MIDDLE OF THE night, completely unrelated to the dream I was having, like a stranger at the door. I saw us there, together. I saw all the colors of the place, shades of greens and yellows, so vivid, and the message in the colors was unmistakable. Aiden had to go there, to Alex, to his grave, and I had to be the one to take him there.

I phoned Aiden right away, and he picked up on the first ring. I told him my plan.

Later, on my morning work break, I phoned Jack, and he gave me directions.

"It's a little tricky. It used to be a horse farm my great uncle owned," Jack told me on the phone. "I almost sold it years ago. But then when Alex passed, I was glad I hadn't. I was happy I could give the family a private place for Alex's ashes, even if it wasn't exactly legal, you know."

Route 101 pointed northward, reaching all the way up through California and Oregon and into Washington State, a part of the old El Camino Real that once linked the Spanish missions, and in parts, hugged the coastline and railroad tracks. But we weren't going that far. First, we passed the outlying sleepy bedroom communities, followed by a succession of suburban shopping malls and outlets on both sides of the highway.

Then there were acres of fields, rows of summer vegetables and berries. A little past Santa Barbara we took the old, two-lane Chumash highway up into the mountains toward Los Olivos. It was cooler there, and I turned off the AC and opened the car windows. The hills were yellow, punctuated only with oak trees, the limbs of the trees leaning across like outstretched arms, even those trees that had been charred from lightning strikes. We passed the Chumash casino, built on the Santa Ynez reservation, and a few miles down the road, I stopped at a roadside fruit stand, and Aiden bought two bunches of flowers.

Back in the car, I almost missed it. There were no road signs, only hard-to-spot landmarks, two pine trees and a large rock, a faded purple ribbon on a chain link fence, followed by an old mailbox, were Jack's instructions. I parked on the cracked driveway of a boarded-up house, and we both got out to walk the half-mile to the site, passing an abandoned stable and a corral.

Aiden had been quiet in the car, quieter still on the path through a hay-yellow meadow. I reached for his hand, and held it as we walked. I spotted the one oak tree and the little lake first, pointing in their direction.

"Is that it?"

"Yes." He was very sure, even though he'd only been there once. "The lake is so low," he said. "It must have lost fifteen feet."

There were rings around the lake, lines where once there had been water. But the tree was exactly as he remembered it, he told me, a California Live Oak, its enormous, web-like limbs spread out wide above the rough piece of stone they had placed there, etched only with Alex's name. Aiden set his flowers down first.

"My mom didn't want his birth date and the day he died engraved on the stone. She said that without the dates, it would be as if there were no measure of the years he'd lived, as though he still existed," Aiden said.

I set down my flowers. "Do you want to say something?" I asked, as we stood over the marker.

Aiden shook his head, no. "I think I just want to sit here for a while."

We sat down in a small patch of grass under the shade of the tree. I hugged my knees, picking up one of the leaves, spiny-toothed with tiny, sharp thistles, cupped and spoon-like. But the leaves seemed so small compared to the enormous tree.

I heard a noise and looked up. There must have been a local airport nearby, because I could hear the buzz of prop planes in the distance, and I thought of our dads.

"I'm glad it's not raining," Aiden suddenly said. "I'm glad it's hot and dry and cloudless. It's weird. It's the first time all summer I'm not wishing for it to rain."

"Tell me more about Alex," and Aiden told me a story about the time Alex rescued a dog from underneath a parked car. The dog didn't want to come out. "But Alex wouldn't let it go, on his belly for an hour, finally luring the dog out with some beef jerky." I laughed hard at the part of the story when Alex ruined his mother's best white guest towels, trying to give the mangy stray a bath, and Aiden laughed with me.

We sat for a while, and Aiden told me other stories. The sun was dropping slowly in the west and Aiden stood up. "I guess we should get going now," he said, but I hesitated.

"Are you sure?" I asked, and he nodded yes, helping me up.

"Thanks for bringing me here."

We'd walked about halfway back, past the stable, when Aiden stopped and turned around.

"I think Alex should have it, don't you?" he asked.

I knew what he meant. He walked quickly back to the tree, and I followed.

"Alex should have it," Aiden repeated. He fell to the ground on his knees, and called out Alex' name. Then he wiped the stone clean with the palm of his hand. He took the book out of his back pocket and set it down near the stone. "Thanks for lending this to me, little bro. It's time to give it back to you," Aiden whispered, opening the book, and leaving it there.

I closed my eyes. And when I opened them, I knew

that what I'd seen wasn't possible, but I could have sworn that in that moment, I saw them, all the ghosts of *Moby Dick*. I saw the whale and the captain, the prophet and the first mate, all flying away from Aiden, like wisps of smoke above a campfire, banished and falling up into the canopy and the embrace of the oak tree.

CHAPTER 31

Leah was clearing off the dining room table when I came home. It was that time of the year again, just a few weeks before the regular school year began, when my mother would sit us down at the table together and have everyone cut up images from magazines for her art class. She'd bring out stacks of magazines and brochures, piles of them she'd collected by going around to the neighbors and doctors' waiting rooms, along with shoeboxes full of special scissors, some for scallops and deckle edges, others with wave patterns.

Leah didn't believe in throwing anything away and Jordan used to love to make fun of her art "shelter." She kept boxes full of stuff in the garage, odds and ends, string and broken window screens, jars of bent nails, pieces of old flooring. "We can give them a new life," she used to say, happy to rescue and recycle scraps from the trash, but sometimes I wondered whether the three of us, Jordan, Gabriela, and me, were also merely throwaways Leah had needed to rescue.

"Oh good, you're home. I could use your help," Leah called out as I passed by in the hallway.

"I just got back. Maybe later."

"You've been avoiding me, Maddie."

I stopped. "Guess I have," and I turned to go upstairs. I was too exhausted from the drive and the afternoon at Alex's grave for a showdown with her.

"You know, this dining room set is one of the few things I kept from my mother," Leah said, running her hand across the table top of dark mahogany. "I used to play under it when I was a child."

"You really want to get into this now? 'Cause I don't." I could hear a soup pot in the kitchen bubbling over, and it caught me off guard. It was too hot for Leah to be making soup.

"I do."

"Okay. Then, let's have it out and now," I said, but first I went into the kitchen to turn off the burner, and Leah followed me. It was the red pot this time, the one she always used for red lentils. The burnt-red liquid had run down the pot. "You explain to me why you didn't tell me about Jordan and Gabriela. You tell me why you didn't think that was important enough to tell me."

I went back into the dining room, Leah at my heels. She looked at me and sighed. "You never knew your grandparents, my parents," Leah said and started organizing the art supplies on the table. "My father was an imposing man, very tall, very handsome, and a good businessman, but he wasn't a good husband, and he was a worse father. I used to hear him talking to my mother about me. He'd laugh and say that I was pretty enough to get married, but stupid, and that Phil got all the smart genes, and there'd been none left for me. He'd tell her that it was all about biology and genetics."

She walked around the table, placing scissors in the middle, and magazines at each chair. "And it hurt, Maddie. It hurt a lot. And my mother, I loved her. She was a good woman, but she could never stand up to him." Leah stopped when she reached the head of the table. "I guess it was then that I swore to myself that when I had children, biology and genetics would never be a factor for me. It would have no importance for me and for them, and when I couldn't have children of my own, I was even more adamant."

Leah looked like she'd run out of air when she finished. She had never spoken much about her parents, who had both passed away long before I was adopted.

"Your father should never have said that to you. You're not stupid."

"For me, it didn't matter that Jordan and Gabriela were related by blood. That was just a coincidence. How could it matter when your father and I changed all that? We reinvented genetics and biology by making something new, a new family. Can you understand, Maddie?"

I leaned over and picked up one of the deckle-edged scissors from the box in the middle of the table.

"That was always my favorite," Leah said.

"Mine too," and I sat down and started flipping through one of the magazines. "Where are all the regular scissors?"

"I put them all away. Nothing is straight edged. Life is too complicated for perfect cuts. I always thought I wanted to paint," Leah said. "But paint has an organic energy. It was too soft for me, like flesh, and I turned to metal. The metal was cold and hard, but somehow I could better understand it. Somehow, with the metal in my hands, it was the first time I felt powerful."

I looked up at her from my magazine. I could smell the lentil soup now, the cumin and coriander. "And why in the world are you making hot soup in this crazy heat?"

"Because it's the best way to cool down," she said.

I looked down again at the magazine. I chose the image I wanted to cut out from it, an orange-yellow sunset. The kids in Leah's class would love the sunset, they always did, this I knew from years of cutting them out for Leah, but I couldn't do it. I couldn't make a cut.

"I just wish you'd have told me," I said, and I got up from the table and went up to bed.

CHAPTER 32

I T WAS THE LAST CLASS OF OUR SIX-WEEK SESSION AND everyone was looking forward to trying out the earthquake simulator the CERT battalion leader had pulled strings to get for us.

Just as I got to the park, Jordan texted me.

"We need to talk," the text said, but the earthquake simulator was arriving atop a long, flatbed truck and I turned off my phone. We all stood and watched as it backed up slowly into the parking lot of the rec center, and I could feel a new energy in our training group.

Outside the simulator, we were divided into three groups of five, and Angela and I were in the first group to walk up the steps and enter.

"Don't wear out the machine for us," someone yelled out to us from the second group, and everyone laughed.

Inside, there was a mock kitchen, a table with five chairs, and a pendant lamp over the table. The cabinets were full of dishes, and pots stood on a stove. A fake window with curtains looked out onto a painted city scene. Plants, books, a computer, and a TV finished off the room.

Someone giggled.

We sat at the table, talking and ribbing each other, expecting the shaking to begin right away, but when our battalion commander closed the door, the room went completely quiet.

We waited.

Five minutes passed, and then another ten. The room started to get hot, and people were getting edgy. Angela got up to try to open the door, but it was jammed shut. She started pounding on the door.

"Let me out, let me out," she said. That's when the shaking started. First, a trembling then an upward and downward movement.

Drop. Cover. Hold on.

Four of us dropped under the table. Angela was still at the door. I got up and grabbed her, pulling her down to the floor. Worse than the shaking and rocking was the rolling, like a ship at sea. The room started to sway, the pendant lamp flying back and forth across the ceiling. The lights went out and we were completely in the dark. Dishes crashed and books fell. Then we heard the sounds of car alarms and sirens.

I was still shaking when the quake seemed to sputter away.

We all got up to leave.

Then it geared up again.

CHAPTER 33

AIDEN AND I BOTH HAD THE DAY OFF, AND I was hoping to spend a whole, uninterrupted day with him. When I sat down in his car, though, I noticed there was something definitely different. His car was neat. There was no diving gear in the back seat, no papers or CDs. *Moby Dick* was gone, left as a memorial on Alex's grave, and it felt good. Today was a clean slate.

"So, what's this all about?"

"Just thought it was about time I cleaned up my act," he smiled. "So, where to today?" he asked.

"It's the last day of summer. Let's go to the beach."

He looked at me strangely. "I thought you hated the beach."

"Not exactly hate. And anyway, it's probably much cooler at the beach, right?

"I'm game," Aiden said and turned the car engine on, taking the freeway north and heading to the ocean.

He exited the freeway at Malibu Canyon, a road that wound slowly up into the Santa Monica Mountains and through a narrow tunnel, and then descended quickly to the ocean. At the top of the crest, I felt it, the edge of humidity in the air, the marine layer washing off the top of the ocean, a tiny drop in temperature, and I rolled down the window to breathe it in.

"I know the best place," he said, his eyes turning sage green, and at the end of the canyon he crossed over Pacific Coast Highway to Malibu Bluff Park. "This is perfect," he said, when we got out of the car, fishing out a camera from the trunk and slinging it over his shoulder.

"Isn't that the one you sold, that first day I met you? You got it back?"

"Jack bought it back for me. When I told him I'd sold it, he marched me back to the camera store, and luckily it hadn't been sold. He also loaned me one of his lenses. Jack says that selling a rare camera like that is like selling your soul."

"I'm so glad you got it back."

We headed in the direction of the shore. First we walked past a couple of bright-green baseball fields sitting on a high promontory. There, closer to the ocean side of the park, stood two telescopes. "Sometimes, if you watch long enough, you can see the blue humpback whales migrating," Aiden said, pointing to the telescopes. "I saw them, the humpbacks, up close, when I was on the Esperanza. So close I even touched them."

"You did?"

"I know a path down to the water." And as the path

zigzagged down to the ocean, he told me about his expedition to the Southern Ocean. "It was less than two years ago," he said. "But it feels like it was someone else's life."

"That first day. You told me about being seasick."

"You remember that?" He laughed. And then he told me about the humpback whales, and his promise to Alex. His words spilled like water over the path, and it was good that the path was long, because with each step we took, I could fill in so many of his pieces, and for once, the world seemed upright.

When we reached the ocean, shimmering in the sun. The sand was full of bright umbrellas. Across the white-hot dunes, someone was unloading blue and white striped mattresses for a private party, and girls were splattered on beach chairs close to the surf. I blinked at the colors, the saturated pigments, reds and oranges, in the bathing suits and towels on the crowded beach. Aiden started to walk faster.

"Where are we going?" I asked a little breathless, trying to keep up with him.

"You'll see," he said, pointing to a distant spot where there was some shade. "We're almost there," he coaxed. "Just a little farther."

We followed the surf west for about twenty minutes, but in the heat I felt as though I was sleepwalking. He walked faster and faster, but guided me easily around the curves of the water, then to a path through rocks flecked with moss. Finally we came to a lagoon, cliffs above.

There was barely a tide, only a soft lapping where the blue of the sky melded with the warm sea. The place looked strangely familiar, and I took off my flip-flops. The sand felt good.

Aiden took a deep breath and looked around. "We can sit over there," he said, and motioned to a shaded area overlooking the water. I sat down to catch my breath, but Aiden was still standing.

"I used to come here every summer. I know every inch, every rock and cove." He took the lens cap off his camera and walked over to the water, taking five or six shots.

"You don't use digitals?"

"I've got one of those too, but this is different. "

I thought about my small digital, its tiny green light flashing on and off, the different sounds it made when I turned it on for either camera mode or view mode, quiet sounds. I could view the photo and immediately delete it, then take another in its place.

Like a lighthouse beacon, he made a 360-degree scan around the entire area. Aiden was taking it all in, absorbing and separating at the same time, deciding what he wanted to keep with him and remember. "These old single lens reflex cameras are pretty amazing. The lens sees the image upside down, and then the mirror turns the image right side up."

"The brain flips the images the eye sees, too."

"Right." Just then he pointed the camera at me and I held up my hand in front of my face.

"Okay, smile."

I made a face.

"C'mon, Maddie."

"I'm not too good at this. I'm better behind the camera." I scrambled for an excuse, still thinking about upside-down images.

"I really want to take your picture," he said.

"Okay," I smiled, and I heard his camera, loud and decisive when the lens clicked, opened, and shut. "Are you using color or black-and-white film?"

"Black and white. It's brutally honest. No colors to soften things up."

"Oh great." I made a face. "Shades of gray. Very flattering."

"Don't worry. It's going to be great," he predicted.

"But you're not going to be able to know that until it's developed and printed."

"It's more interesting that way, not knowing the outcome. It's a leap of faith, Maddie," he said, and set his camera down atop a flattened rock. "I'm going for a dip. Want to come in?"

"I didn't bring a bathing suit."

"It doesn't matter."

"No thanks. You go ahead." It was nice to be here with Aiden, but I was edgy near the ocean.

He looked disappointed and I watched him as he ran down to the water's edge. While he was running, he peeled off his shirt, diving into the foamy surf. Even from a distance I could see he looked different in the water. I was watching him but also watching the water, the way it reached onto the shore and then retreated. It was a shiny glaze of color, and it seemed safe for once, the certainty of the water's ebb and flow.

When Aiden came out of the surf, his body was sleek as a seal, and his hair was dripping wet. He was holding a fistful of wet plastic bags he'd found bubbling to the surface in the surf.

"Marine animals think they're jellyfish, and choke on these damn things," he said, tying up the wet bags.

"But they're everywhere."

"They don't have to be," he said, dumping the bags into a nearby trashcan

He stretched out on the sand near me. The sun was warm on his face and soon his eyes grew sleepy. He closed them and I watched his chest rise and fall, his hands soft against the sand and I curled up against him, my head tucked in between his neck and shoulder. His skin smelled salty, and I traced my fingertips on his lips. I was sleepy too, and I whispered in his ear, "Love you."

Drowsy, he turned over in the sand to me, reaching over, pulling me in closer. "Love you," he whispered back sleepily. His hand moved slowly down from my face, and under my shirt to my breasts, caressing them. Half asleep, his kisses on my lips felt different now, no longer careful, and then I kissed him on the hollow of his chest. But the sun beat down on us. A thick gauze of layered light wrapped around my eyelids, and soon we were both deep in sleep.

When I woke up, I was startled to see Aiden, dressed and sitting upright, looking out at the water. My eyes were barely focused, but I could see a family of dolphins riding the surf close to shore. They arced in and out of the waves, playing in the foam. Then I heard something, someone whistling, but it sounded far away.

"They say it's bad luck to whistle on a ship. A whistle challenges the wind and brings on a storm."

"Guess it's good we're not on a ship," I tried to joke, barely awake.

"The seabed drops down off the shore a couple of miles out. It falls like a cliff," Aiden said, his eyes intent on the water.

"What?" I was still sluggish, almost dreaming his words, when he stood up abruptly.

"Got to watch out for the undertow. It will pull you down, and you won't even feel it."

"What?" I asked again. All I heard was the word undertow.

"Maybe this was a mistake? Maybe we shouldn't have come here?" His voice was full of regret.

"What? Why?" I could hardly understand what he was saying. I closed my eyes, and the sun burned red on my eyelids.

"Being here, this isn't right. It isn't fair to you."

"I don't understa—" I looked to the ocean, but the shimmer had dissolved into matte.

"We should go," he said, as he helped me get up. He started walking back in the direction of his parked car. "I can't fall in love with you now, Maddie. I can't fall in love with anyone now. I have to figure out my life first."

There was a horrible lump in my throat, but I held back tears. "We can figure it out together."

"I'm sorry, Maddie. I'm so sorry, but I have to do this myself. It's the only way."

"'I have to do this myself?'" I mimicked him. "That's too easy." But I couldn't stop the tears that now started to roll down my cheeks.

He kissed the tears away on my face. "Easy? No, Maddie, my love. What would be easy is to love you and make love to you, but that wouldn't be fair. It wouldn't be right. I don't want to make the same mistakes."

"But we're not the mistake. We're not the one-night stand. And we're not on a ship in the middle of the Southern Ocean," I yelled at him.

He kissed me again. "I'm sorry. I'm so sorry. But I can't, I can't," he repeated. He took my hand, and suddenly I was on the path back, not knowing how I got there, just like that first day when he took my hand and guided me out of the camera store.

I let go of his hand. On the way to the car, the sand under my feet felt dried out, burning up, like my head. It reminded me of the place Leah had brought me one summer, the place where we'd come across the body of a beached dolphin lying in the sand, and my legs buckled for a moment beneath me.

We reached his car. "I need something to drink." I was parched, but I was also desperate to slow down time.

"Sure, we'll stop somewhere," he said, and we stopped at a mini mart on Pacific Coast Highway.

We walked in together and ordered a couple of large sodas from a self-serve dispenser. It was cool in the store, but there was nowhere to sit. My head was pounding by now and I just wanted to sit down.

"We could sit in the car," I suggested, after he paid for the sodas at the register. I took a big gulp and nearly choked on my drink.

"Too hot in the car," he said, looking around for somewhere to sit outside in the shade, and there was only one long, wobbly-looking bench. We sat down and tears welled up in my eyes again.

I looked down to see an empty coffee cup lying sideways on the floor. The last bits of liquid had left a pattern, like rings on a tree stump. There were two overly watered trees in pots on both sides of the bench, and two trickles of liquid led from the pots to the parking lot. I wanted to reach across the bench and touch Aiden, but he didn't say a word, and despite the heat, I shivered, hugging my arms.

"Maybe we should just go?"

"Not yet," Aiden said. "Just a little while longer."

"Then let's not stay here, let's go back to the beach."
I wanted to return there, with him, feel the sand and the
water, fall asleep beside him. I wanted to reshoot the
scene—he would ask me to take a swim with him again,
and this time I would say yes. I'd put aside my fears and
follow him into the water, but he just shook his head.

He stood up. "I left something in the car. I'll be back
in a minute." Five, long minutes later, though, he returned with a large envelope.

"I've been wanting to give this to you," Aiden said,
handing it to me.

"What's this?" I stammered.

"They're letters. I want you to have them."

I started to open the envelope clasp when he put his
hand over mine. "Not now. Read them only before you
go to New York."

"New York?"

I wanted to tell him about Miles being broke, about
the fact that I'd come to the decision not to go, but I
couldn't get the words out, and I thought about New York
City, building alongside building, block after colorless
block. "What about you? Have you made up your mind?"

He turned a fraction toward me, his voice low and
bleak. "It's not just about the rest of my life and taking
responsibility, but more about what would be good for
her, for Hope. Something good should have happened
out of all this by now," he said, wistfully. "If this was
really meant to be."

"Something good did happen," I offered, but the words rang hollow in my mouth. "We happened."

Just then a man left the market with a cart full of food, juggling two hot cups. Suddenly, he lost his grip on his cart and it rolled away down an incline, heading directly to a parked car.

Aiden jumped up and ran after the cart, but he was too late to grab the handle and the cart slammed into the front fender of the car.

"Hey, thanks for trying, man," the guy said to Aiden, but Aiden only shrugged. He turned to me and looked me squarely in the eye. "You see, I'm still cursed."

I quickly surveyed the damage. "But there's hardly a dent."

We walked back to the bench

Later, in the car, we talked about meeting up the next day, and Aiden said he would call me. He took the canyon road back toward the valley and I turned around to look out the back window. I was holding on to the envelope he'd given me, but I was also trying to hold on to the edge of the blue horizon of water disappearing through the window. It became smaller and smaller, the color diluted and washed out, until there was no blue left.

January 13, 2008

Dear Alex—

Humane Starbuck was too late.

*You underlined that phrase in the book, then copied
it, and taped it up to the wall above your bed. You said it
was a good reminder that you never wanted to look back
and say that you were too late.*

*And now, despite all our efforts, in spite of
everything, one of the hunter ship's harpoons reaches a
target. We were too late for her.*

*How do I describe the blood? There's so much of it.
All I can see is the color red. Even fathoms of seawater
can't dilute the red stain, and the ocean is choking with
blood. The numbers tell us we've succeeded in saving the
rest of the pod, but it's no comfort. What do numbers
mean if we lost even one?*

*The harpoon gunnery is larger than I imagined and it
looks like artillery on a battleship. But this war is very
different. The harpoon shoots, carefully aiming to hit
behind the blowhole, and thirty seconds later, the grenade
explodes inside the whale.*

Inside.

*I think about the whale and her calf we saw the other
day. What if this whale was carrying a calf? The thought
doesn't leave me.*

*But she doesn't die right away. She fights to extricate
herself from the harpoon line, and they reload. I see the
line from the ship to the whale, the scurry of men when the
second harpoon hits its target again.*

They reel her in and strap her tail to the side of the ship, dragging her alongside, head down in the water, but she's still alive. We bring our inflatable boat as close as we can.

But we can only watch, helpless, the terrible sight. She looks at us, and her eye asks "Why?" I reach out to touch her. The whale won't die immediately. She will die slowly, eventually too weak to lift her head to breathe. It takes her forty minutes to drown, to suffocate, and a piece of me dies with her.

Forgive me if I can't write anything else down. Forgive me if I don't want to remember what I've seen.

Forgive me, Alex.

Al – ways –
Aiden

CHAPTER 34

'D JUST LEFT THE SUPERMARKET AND WAS ABOUT TO
get into my car, I'd never been so tired in my life.
Every inch of my body ached, every muscle, every bone. I
felt as though I was being dragged down, like Aiden had
said, into an undertow, but he was wrong about not feeling it. I felt it pulling me. I reached into my tote bag
where I'd kept Aiden's envelope, then stopped.

Read the letters only before you go to New York, he'd
said, a long week ago, the last time I'd seen or spoken
with him.

But I wasn't going to New York, and I put the envelope back in the tote.

My phone rang. It was Leah. She'd left five cheery
voicemail messages on my cell, none of which I'd had the
energy to listen to. I was about to turn off my phone
when it rang again.

"Maddie, I've been trying to reach you for days. I
have to talk to you."

My eyes were burning, but the voice was so familiar.
Aiden?

It was Jordan. I hadn't seen him almost two months, since that July morning at the nature reserve, and he sounded worried.

"Is something wrong? Did you do something to screw up your probation? I can't really talk. This isn't really a good time for me."

"Everything's okay. I just want to see you. You didn't answer my phone call and my text. I've been wanting to talk to you about going to New York."

I told him I already knew our parents were broke, and that I'd decided not to go to New York. "Anyway, since when are you Mom and Dad's messenger?"

"That's not what I mean. I wanted to tell you that you should go."

"What?"

"Actually, you have to go."

"What are you saying, Jordan?" I asked, and it was the first time he didn't correct me.

"You have to go even if Mom and Dad can't pay for it."

"That doesn't even make any sense, and anyway it's too late."

"It's not too late." He'd done some research about rolling admissions, scholarship money and student loans. His words were slow and deliberate. "And there's lots of resources out there for you."

"Not happening."

"It's not like you to give up. Please come with me. I want you to see something. I know what you're thinking.

But everything's different now. And I want you to be the first to see what I'm doing. I'll pick you up and I promise I'll get you back to your car in no more than an hour."

"All right," I finally agreed.

Jordan picked me up in a used car he'd just bought. In the car, I noticed that there was something very different about him. He'd stopped shaving his head, his chestnut brown hair growing in like peach fuzz, and one of the tattoos on his right arm had been lasered off and was healing.

Ten minutes later he stopped the car in back of a five-story medical building. The back door was locked, but he produced a key from his pocket

"The classes I was trying to tell you about . . . they're about radiology, you know . . . to become a radiology technician."

"Radiology?"

"Maddie. I really like what I'm doing," Jordan said, as we walked through the empty lobby toward the elevators. He keyed the elevator to the third floor. "The 3-D scans are amazing. I really think I finally found what I want to do," he said, and I hadn't seen him so excited in years.

When we reached the third floor, Jordan unlocked the door to what looked like a lab. The waiting room was dark, but he knew his way to the light switch.

"Wait here," he said, and he disappeared into another room, returning with a handful of black and white films. "Look at these ultrasounds."

I looked at them and imagined the sound waves becoming images, soft organs and living tissues, beautiful babies floating in a pool of amniotic fluid. The images weren't just on the film, but were also reflected in Jordan's eyes. "But what about Dad? He needs me to help out, especially now."

"I'll watch out for Miles."

"You?"

"I worked it out with Mom and Dad, and we've been actually talking, Maddie, really talking for once. Things aren't perfect, but they're getting better. Let me talk to Dad about New York for you. I know I can make him understand."

I looked at my brother's face and started to cry.

"I can't. I can't go now."

"You have to. Remember our trip to Guatemala when we were kids? Remember what the flight attendant said?"

"I don't understand."

"You know . . . the instructions we all made fun of before takeoff? If the cabin loses pressure and the oxygen masks fall down, they tell the adults to place their masks on first, to breathe in and then fit the masks on the children. We thought it was stupid, but they were right. You have to save yourself before you can save anyone else, Maddie."

Jordan reached over and held me tight, and I felt safe with him in the lab. "I don't know."

"I'm sorry you had to find out about me and Gabriela

the way you did, Maddie. Mom and Dad should have told you."

"I wish they had. And Gabriela, did she know? Did you know?""

"We both didn't know. They only told us after you found out. They're really sorry. Mom was so upset." Jordan let go of me, then walked over to a desk and handed me something. "Here's an extra ultrasound photo I saved for you, one that got jammed up in the machine. It's something no one would want, no one except you."

I looked at the black-and-white ultrasound photo, white lettering and numbers on the edges. It was a little creased, but only nuanced by the folds, and the arced triangle swirled with a living being.

"It's so beautiful." Tears kept streaming down my face. "Thank you. Thank you."

"I have to tell you something else, Maddie."

"What?" I blinked away my tears.

"The reason I violated probation that time." Jordan said quietly. "It wasn't what you think. And it wasn't you. I did it on purpose. I wanted to go back to jail."

"What are you saying?"

"I wasn't safe at that placement, and they wouldn't believe me when I told them what happened there, and there was no other way I could think of."

I looked into Jordan's eyes and understood.

I'd overheard my parents' whisperings about things

that happened at some placements, bits and pieces of conversations, about older boys who took advantage of the younger ones. At the time, Jordan's violating his probation made no sense. He'd been doing well in school, everything was going right, and then suddenly, there had been a terrible hurt and anger in his eyes.

"The worst part, was that no one believed me. Not the house manager, not my PO, no one."

"You should have told me."

"I'd done so much lying by then. Would you have believed me?"

"I'm so sorry. I'm so sorry. You should have told me, and I should have believed you. I shouldn't have said what I said. I shouldn't have told you to run away."

"It's done now, it's over. I just wanted you to know, Maddie. I'm okay."

"Okay," I repeated. Jordan was okay. I could see him clearly now. Like one of the impressionist paintings I'd seen in a museum, I'd stood too close to really see him. He'd only been a blur of dots of paint. Stepping back, now, I could see that he was whole again.

"I'll call you tonight."

"Okay . . . Jorge."

"You don't have to call me that if you don't want to."

"But I want to. I really do, Jorge," I said, and he drove me back to my car.

Later, at home in my bedroom I tried texting Aiden but he didn't respond. Then I tried calling him but his phone didn't even ring. It went immediately to voice mail, and it wasn't even his voice.

I hung up.

I thought about Jorge and his radiology classes. I walked over and knocked on Gabriela's bedroom door.

"I was thinking that Jorge never got his birthday cake," I said. "I thought I'd get one of those big cakes at the supermarket and we could drive over and give it to him."

"Jorge? You said Jorge?"

"Yes."

Gabriela jumped up from her desk and hugged me. "Yes. Let's make sure it's his favorite. You know, German chocolate, with coconut," Gabriela chirped. "And let's make sure it's three layers. One layer for each of us," Gabriela said, running down the stairs.

"Yes. German chocolate cake. Three layers."

We left a note for Leah, and headed out to Jorge's placement.

Outside, night was replacing the last strands of twilight. Jorge's placement in East LA was less than twenty miles away, but it was a part of town I'd never been to. I got lost switching from the 101 Freeway to Interstate 5, which circled madly around downtown. My hands trembled a little on the steering wheel as I was driving on the dark freeway. There were long stretches of graffiti and fluorescent lights, and unfamiliar freeway exits, but Gabriela was smiling next to me in the front seat, our store-bought chocolate cake neatly boxed up on her lap.

"Jorge will be so, so happy," Gabriela said, humming to herself, and he was. He greeted us at the door with giant bear hugs, and showed us around the first floor of the smallish halfway house, introducing us to some of the residents, then took us upstairs to his room.

"We brought you your birthday cake," Gabriela announced, handing him the cake box.

"Birthday? I think that was a while ago," he laughed.

"But it's not too late for a belated birthday cake," I chimed in, and I noticed some packing boxes in his room. "What's going on?"

"I guess I forgot to tell you. I'm moving back home next week," Jorge said. "My PO made the recommendation and Mom and Dad both agreed."

"They did? You're coming home?" Gabriela jumped up on Jorge's back and he twirled her around and around until they both fell on the floor, laughing.

"That's the best news, Jorge," and I started cutting up large slabs of cake while Jorge poured sodas. We sat in his room, surrounded by his moving boxes. The boxes were from Miles's store, the last of his inventory, perfect rectangles, sealed and ready to go. And it didn't take long for all three of us, even Gabriela, to finish every lick of frosting, every last crumb of chocolate cake, like small slices of hope.

CHAPTER 35

THE NEXT MORNING I DIDN'T KNOW WHAT TO DO with myself. I paced around in my room for awhile, then got in the car. I drove past the camera store first then to the park, and walked over to the picnic table where Aiden had played chess with Jack. After that, I went to the movie theater, the spot near Capitol Records and the dam, trying to retrace some of our steps together, even the last stops on the bus tour we'd been ejected from, and the beach. I didn't really know what I expected to find in these places, certainly not Aiden, but maybe a remnant that could help reconstruct what had gone wrong. But there was nothing in all those places, not a shred, nothing in the air or the streets, as though every faint suggestion of him was gone.

The digital car clock showed 8:01 p.m. I'd driven for hours, zigzagging across Los Angeles, and I was sapped by the time I pulled over. There were no signs of him anywhere, only the words he'd tossed out at me with the wind on the beach.

Maybe this just isn't meant to be.

Only seven words, but sharp and precise as the slit of the X-Acto knives I used to cut scraps.

The traffic on Ventura Boulevard buzzed east and west and I decided to park the car and walk for a while. The nighttime temperature had finally dropped into the low 80s, and it was a balmy evening. I passed a flower store, closed for the night, walking beneath an arch of deflated balloons strung up from the store to a lamppost on the street. I'd walked less than a couple of blocks when I noticed a small corner house across the street. It had a bright, white picket fence and a neat lawn, and if there hadn't been a neon sign in the window, I wouldn't have guessed what was inside.

"Psychic Sonia," the neon sign advertised in a purplish hue, while giant, painted tarot cards formed a screen at the entrance. Another neon sign blinked "Open," and I stopped. I wanted a better look, but there was no crosswalk, and I decided to make a run for it across the busy boulevard.

Closer now, I could see a dried-out fountain and a statue of an angel, the angel's hand outstretched. I stood by the picket gate and was about to gauge how many footsteps it would take to get to the doorway, when I stopped myself, mid-calculation, and walked up the path to ring the doorbell. No one answered, so I rang again. I was about to turn around and leave when a barefoot woman wearing a pair of faded jeans came to the door, her long, dark hair loosely tied to the side with a scarf.

"Come in," she offered. "Sorry about the delay. I was putting my kid to bed." The woman smelled of cinnamon and saffron, but just like her clothing, the room beyond the doorway wasn't anything like what I'd expected. There were no oriental rugs and tasseled curtains or crystals hanging from the ceiling, only a couple of simple couches and a coffee table, and floor-to-ceiling bookcases lining the walls.

"Yeah. I don't go for that whole fortune teller look," the woman said. "I don't believe in 'atmosphere.'"

"Oh."

"Either you got the gift or not. It all started with my grandmother," Sonia began. "She was from Spain. She taught me how to fly out of my body at night and find lost things. I'd wake up in the morning and know exactly where to find a lost key or a hat." She stopped, looking for my reaction, then continued. "I used to work full time painting scenery for movie sets, you know, fake backdrops, facades without anything behind them. Anyway, one day . . . I like . . . you know . . . had a moment. Guess you could call it one of those revelations? Anyway, I knew it was time to quit. That life wasn't me. You got to know yourself, right?"

"Sure," I said.

"So, why are you here? What do you need to know?" She said, ushering me into the living room. We sat down at a small table.

A hundred questions rang loudly in my head, but

only one, odd query came to me. "Why are psychics almost always women?"

Sonia looked at me and smiled. "That's what you want to know? But I think you know the answer to that one."

"I don't."

Sonia smiled again and leaned lightly against the doorjamb. "We're the ones who give birth and dream our baby's dreams. No man can do that. I can tell you everything you want to know . . . about him too."

"Him?"

"It's about him really, right? You want to know whether it's meant to be."

I touched the edge of the greenstone pendant I was wearing.

"He's the one who gave you the necklace you're wearing, isn't he?"

I was happy she was wrong. "No, he didn't, actually. It was my uncle who brought it back for me from one of his trips, to New Zealand."

Sonia thought a moment. "That's it," she said. "That's the connection. It's New Zealand. *Pounamu* is the Maori name for the greenstones they carve. That's why I felt it was *him*. He was there too."

"I don't understand." But looking down closely at the stone, I saw there were small veins of white I hadn't noticed before, little tributaries flowing in all directions. And then I remembered. Aiden had told me that his ship, the *Esperanza*, had left from New Zealand.

She looked at me closely. "I don't only do tarot readings. I can do auras too. I have an aura imaging camera."

I hesitated again. I'd read about aura simulation cameras. First, a photograph of the person was taken, then a hand sensor measured the electromagnetic field around the person and would be superimposed on the first photo, the clouds of colors representing different states of being.

"No, I don't really want to see my aura."

"Just look," and Sonia reached for a photograph from a stack on the table. "See this? The colors of the energy field reflect our emotions and state of consciousness."

I looked at the photo. The aura surrounding the person was egg-shaped, a blend of colors melting into each other, barely revealing a softly obscured face. Everything was beautiful in soft focus, all flaws rubbed away. But at that moment, I wanted to see myself in sharp focus, like the black-and-white photos Aiden had taken of me on the beach, the photographs I would never see. "It's really okay. I have to go."

"I see."

I dug into my pocket, but came up empty. "Sorry, but I left my money in my car. I can't pay you."

"That's all right, dear," she said at the door. She looked out to the street. "Looks like there's a good breeze out there now, a nice, mild one" she said, and closed the door.

Driving home, the tops of the palm trees were swaying in a light wind. I was almost home when a single plastic bag floated up from the street, landing on my windshield. I turned on the wipers and drove a few more blocks, but the bag wouldn't detach, and I pulled over to peel it off. The bag was practically new, the same talc-white kind we gave out hundreds of times a day at the supermarket. Miles would have said it was just a random, statistical probability, a meaningless event from which I shouldn't extrapolate a conclusion. But Aiden's meant to be was still stuck in my head.

I wadded up the plastic bag into a small ball and threw it into the backseat then headed to the supermarket, and backed my car up against the loading dock. I opened my trunk and left it open, using my employee card key to go through the back entrance. I saw the wooden pallet, stacked three feet high with cartons of plastic bags. I knew there was no one in the storeroom at that time of night, but I had to work fast. It didn't take me long to make about a dozen trips back and forth between the storeroom and my car. I knew I couldn't take them all, and someone would reorder them tomorrow. I had no idea what I would do with them, but I took as many as I could fit in my trunk—six cartons, three thousand bags in each carton that wouldn't end up in the ocean—shut the trunk, and drove away.

CHAPTER 36

STILL NOTHING FROM AIDEN, AND I COULD SMELL it even before I was fully awake, the strong odor of ash and smoke. Yesterday, the temperature had tied with the highest on record, and the fires were getting closer. A hundred thousand acres had already burned, even sections of nearby West Hills were smoldering and some homes were being evacuated. I turned on the TV in the den and saw the news. Fire planes sprayed pinkish fire retardant into a sky where the black smoke had turned day into night.

My parents had driven down to San Diego with Gabby for a couple of days, Jorge hadn't moved back in yet, and I was alone in the house. I dressed very slowly, taking my time. My skin felt raw to the touch, every muscle aching. On the dresser was my CERT diploma, and next to that the photo red light ticket I'd gotten in the mail. I looked at the photo closely. It was fuzzy, just like I was feeling. My phone rang and it was Jorge, asking to meet up at the park.

I groggily calculated that the park was less than a mile away, and I agreed.

On my way out of the bedroom, I saw the remnants of a collage I'd been working on. The pieces were still strewn, unconnected on the desk. It was Miles who'd told me that the right brain looked at the whole picture and then the details, while the left brain focused on sequence, looking first at pieces then putting them together to make a whole. I stood over the desk and moved some of the photos and scrap pieces around, first bringing them closer, then placing them further apart. I added a new element, a perfectly coiled inner spring of an old watch I'd found, but still, nothing was gelling, and neither part of my brain was seeing anything. I took the spring, threw it on the floor, and headed out.

When I got to the park, I sat down at one of the picnic tables.

Jorge appeared a few minutes later and swung one leg over the seat of the bench.

"I hope you won't be mad at me . . . but I made some phone calls for you," he started.

"What do you mean?"

"I did some research. That stuff you said about your birthparents. I knew it couldn't be true."

"What stuff? What are you talking about?" Even though it was still early morning, the concrete table was hot to the touch.

"What you said about them giving you up because

you were their fourth child. I called your birth mother, Alma."

"What?" I shouted.

"Just hear me out."

"I don't want to hear it." The table was radiating heat but I fought back a shiver. Somewhere, far off, I heard the sound of a tennis ball being smacked back and forth across a cement court, and it grew louder and louder, while Jorge's face ebbed slowly away. My thoughts were so scattered I thought I was hallucinating.

"They didn't give you up because of numbers, Maddie. They gave you up because their third child was very sick and died because they didn't have the right medical care. And they didn't want that to happen to you."

A tiny wind kicked up the dust, scattering it all around me like particles floating in space. I tried to follow their path with my eyes, but that only made me dizzier. "I can't believe you did that," I yelled at him again, but my own voice sounded just as distant and lost as the tennis ball. I rested my head on the table.

"Did you hear me? Did you hear what I just said? I thought it would make you happy to know the reason they gave you up was for your benefit, so that if you got sick too, you'd have the best medical care."

"Happy?" I was trying so hard to concentrate and make sense of what Jorge was telling me, but my head was hurting, whirling around aimlessly like space junk in the atmosphere. "How can it be true? Mom never said anything about Alma and Raphael's third baby dying."

"Our parents never knew. Your birthparents were afraid to tell them. They thought Mom and Dad wouldn't want to adopt you if they knew their third child had died."

"This is crazy. I can't listen to this. I gotta go," and I stood up, but my legs refused to cooperate and my eyes fluttered back, the trees passing slowly in a blur tinged with washes of color.

A trick photograph I'd seen in a book the other day became fixed in my mind. It was a simple photo of a long hallway with many doors, and people leaning out into the hallway. But once rotated, the photo looked as though the people were hanging from the ceiling.

And then everything turned black. A hundred images flashed before me in rapid succession—my parents dancing in the backyard, Jorge's ultrasound machine, alive and breathing with heartbeats, and Aiden, running out to the edge of the water.

"I got-ta—" I tried to repeat, but the words remained slurred in my mouth.

Suddenly, I was in a bubble. I was floating up and down on a slow motion trampoline. Flashes of light jumped out at me then I was spinning, like planets orbiting in circles, as I hurtled headlong, freefalling into the ground. Finally I landed, and it was the strangest thing. There was the taste of pine needles and blood stinging in my mouth.

"Maddie?" someone said, close to my ear. "Maddie, are you all right?" I recognized Jorge's voice.

"What . . . what happened?" I asked, barely able to speak.

"You gave me a real scare. But it was so lucky," Jorge panted. "This woman here, she's also an ER nurse. She came right over, and she thinks you have some kind of vertigo, maybe from an ear infection."

"Vertigo?" I saw an indistinct shadow of color, a face above me, and I tried to lift up my head, but it felt like a bowling ball.

"Don't get up yet," the woman said, her hand on my wrist. "Looks like she's okay," she continued, taking my pulse. "Just a big scrape on her left temple. A cut to the head may bleed more because those areas have a lot of blood vessels, but it doesn't look like it needs stitches."

"Blood vessels," I repeated. I could still taste the blood that had dripped down my cheek.

"Should I call 911?" Jorge asked.

"No. Don't call. Don't call," I cried. "I'm okay, I'm okay, really."

Jorge didn't look convinced.

"I think she's going to be all right," the woman said. "But make sure she gets checked out," she directed Jorge then patted the top of my hand.

Someone brought over a bottle of water, and I managed to sit up slowly. Jorge held the bottle above my temple and poured it on my cut. "Feeling okay? She thinks you'll do even better after some medication," he told me, still alarmed.

"How could she even know what was the matter with me?" I asked weakly, but I was happy to see that the trees and the tent were upright again.

"Because of the last thing you said to me before you keeled over."

"What did I say?" I asked, still in a daze. I looked down and saw my shirt was stained with blood and water.

"You kept saying, 'I'm falling.'"

January 14, 2008

Dear Alex—

Today, the sky is cloudless, and there isn't a breath of wind, not even near the railing of top deck. It's called a dead calm, when the anemometer measures a wind of less than one knot, and it feels like the world is standing still again, like it did that day.

I should have been a better brother, and a better friend to you. I envied the good grades you brought home and your perfect report cards. I was jealous of the easy way you knew exactly what you wanted and who you wanted to be. So I gave you a hard time, and locked my door to keep you out when my friends came over. I ratted you out to Dad more times than I can remember, even though I was the one who usually egged you on to do stupid things.

I was in the den that day, a long, summer day that didn't want to end.

I was there when I thought I heard a siren, but I wasn't sure, so I didn't put the joystick down. I was almost there, at level four, maneuvering through streets and alleys in a speeding car, obstacles and men with rifles. But soon the siren became louder and louder, and suddenly I didn't hear it in my ears anymore. It rang somewhere else inside my head, in my chest and in my gut, and I ran out the front door screaming your name.

A small crowd had gathered by the time I got to you. You were on the pavement, your bike crushed nearby. Strange, there was hardly a scratch on you; only a small trickle of blood from your ear, and for one crazy moment I

thought it was the sound of the siren that had shattered
your eardrum.

The paramedics were already working on you,
pumping your chest. Your eyes were closed, but I felt you
could still see me and hear me. Then you squeezed my hand
and said my name.

In a long minute, you were on a gurney and then
inside the ambulance, and time stopped. I sat beside you as
the ambulance raced to the hospital. There was no air in
the tomb of the ambulance, and time and wind rushed past
us along with the streets through the window. The IV
dripped, transparent, into your veins. And as you ebbed
away from me, I prayed I would disappear too.

Al – ways –
Aiden

CHAPTER 37

JORGE DROVE ME TO A NEARBY URGENT CARE CLINIC
where the doctor gave me antibiotics for my ear infection. I took my first dose and went to bed early that
night, Jorge sleeping on the couch in my bedroom. But
in the morning he got a call from his fire crew. The volunteer crew had been called up to help out with a new
brush fire in the hills west of the valley.

"You sure you're going to be okay if I leave?" he
asked.

"I'm sure."

I felt better and went downstairs with him while he
grabbed a quick bite to eat. When he left, I sat down at
the kitchen table. It felt good to say the words out loud.

Numbers had nothing to do with it.

Numbers had nothing to do with giving me up.

I turned on the TV in the kitchen. There was a news
report from the fire line explaining how the fire crews
were digging trenches and setting controlled burns. Two
firefighters had already been overcome with smoke.

I tried to call Jorge, but his phone went to voicemail,

and my text to him remained undelivered when my phone buzzed with a text from Bryn.

"Srrrry, Maddie."

Way too late, Bryn.

"It's Gaelic," Bryn texted again, seconds later. "It means 'little fire.'"

"What are you talking about? I texted her back.

"His name, Aiden's name. It means 'little fire.'"

"His name? How do you know his name? We haven't talked and you haven't answered even one of my texts."

"I called up your mom," she texted. "She told me."

A little fire.

A little fire sometimes burns bright, and sometimes smolders away. Bryn was right about people living up to their names. That was him. That was exactly Aiden.

I filled up a large glass of iced water, and sank into an armchair near the window in the living room. Everything seemed surreal, the meds still making me a little sleepy.

My cell rang. Bryn again.

"Are you okay? Jorge called and told me about you fainting in the park, and I've been so worried about you. Where are you now?" she asked.

"Why?"

"Where are you? I'm coming to you," Bryn said, her words crackly, and I could tell she was driving. "I really want to see you," she pleaded.

"Why now?

"Maddie, please," she appealed again. "Please," she begged, and I didn't have the energy to stand up to her sudden insistence.

Fifteen minutes later, Bryn knocked on the front door, her face full of regret.

I stood at the door. "It's too late for this, Bryn, and I'm really tired."

"It can't be too late. I'm so sorry, Maddie." She opened her arms wide and hugged me, her white terry-cloth jacket also soft with apologies, and I let her in. She curled up next to me on the sofa in the living room. "It's so insanely stupid, I know," she said, in a gush of words. "But I guess I've been trying to get used to it, and even way before this summer."

"Used to what?"

"Used to you going away, and not being here anymore," she said, leaning over and gathering me up again in a long hug. "I didn't know what I was going to do with you in New York, and me here . . . without you. And I thought if I kind of let go of you, you know . . . get used to you not being around, it would be easier. It's like what I used to do before my dad went on all those doctor conferences of his . . . I would just kind of detach. Do you understand?"

"I guess."

"Forgive me?"

Bryn didn't seem to notice that I didn't answer.

"You know, for the first time, I actually believe it's

going to happen. I actually believe I'm going to gradu-
ate," she chirped, and I remembered the nights Bryn
would cry herself to sleep.

"I know you will, Bryn."

"Did you know that the word 'bryn' is a Welsh word
for 'hill'? I mean how perfect is that? I've been trying to
climb up my mother's hills forever haven't I, Maddie?"
Bryn laughed. "But you can't get to the top unless you
forgive the hill for making you do the climb." She
laughed again.

"Forgive the hill?" I repeated. "That has to be the
smartest thing you've ever said. I guess I do forgive you."

"I knew you would," Bryn said, and settled deeper
into the sofa, pulling up both her legs, and I did the
same. We were cushion-to-cushion, and I told her about
Aiden and everything that had happened since the day
the water main broke.

"All that lovely wooziness this summer wasn't love,
Bryn, just a plain old ear infection."

"I'm not so sure about that," Bryn said, resting her
chin on her hand.

"I don't know. I just can't let it end like this. I have to
do something."

"But do what?"

I got up from the sofa. "Come and help me?"

"Sure," Bryn said, and we went to the detached garage at the back of the house and turned on the lights.
Bryn helped me clear off a part of Leah's old workspace,

and then I ran upstairs to my bedroom to get the scraps I'd collected over the summer.

When I came back down, the garage was stifling, but I wanted to start on it immediately. It was already there in my head, more complex than any of the other pieces I'd constructed. I felt the textures of the papers beneath my fingers, the strokes of color, the way the piece would eventually sit and become one with the canvas.

Bryn sat on the other workbench, her feet dangling, watching me, but after a while, I almost forgot she was there. First was the fragment Aiden had given me from *Moby Dick*.

The torn-off page was almost sepia.

I started with a clean wood panel then stretched cotton across, stapling the fabric to the back. I could already see how the glue would make the assemblage transparent, how it would find its way into the other scraps I'd collected, and I began. Along with Aiden's torn-off page were the corners of Bryn's photos, cutouts I'd made of a helix of numbers, spiraling across the canvas in sequence, equations, the napkin from the movie theater, and the curled, arcing rim of the paper cup I'd found in the courthouse parking lot. Then there were unexpected elements that came to me, and I added clippings from a magazine, visions of the Yucatan, the Guatemalan rainforest and the bush, Mayan ghosts, and volcanoes.

I was sweating and my hands were shaking.

"Looks great," Bryn said.

I stepped back a couple of feet and shook my head. "No, there's still something missing, and I can't figure it out."

"Really, Maddie, it looks so good." Bryn tried to convince me.

"No. It doesn't work."

All of a sudden, the garage door slowly opened. First, I saw the suitcases, then my parents and then Gabriela.

"Maddie? I'm so glad you're home," Leah cried out, her heartbeat pulsing in her neck. "Jorge called us and we were so worried. You didn't pick up. You okay?" Leah asked, and reached out to hug me.

I nodded. "Have you heard from Jorge?" I asked. "I've been trying to reach him all day."

"I just got off the phone with him. His crew had it rough, but he's okay. The fire's eighty-percent contained, and he said he'll be home in an hour," Leah said, and I breathed a sigh of relief.

Jorge is okay.

"What's this?" Miles asked, looking down at my collage.

"I can't finish it," I said.

Gabriela put her arm around my shoulder. "I like it."

"Me too," Miles offered.

"No, it's unfinished," I persisted.

"I can see now what Maddie's saying," Bryn added.

Part of me wanted to laugh out loud. I'd never had my family stand around and weigh in on one of my collages.

Leah took a closer look, narrowing her eyes. I'd seen that look before, the times she'd stood for hours, evaluating and thinking, in front of her own sculptures.

"It just needs one simple, last element," she opined, taking two steps back, then stepping forward again. Leah was in her element, so familiar with rescue missions. Then the thoughtful frown line that had burrowed in her forehead suddenly disappeared.

"I know I've got it somewhere around here," Leah declared and vanished into the house. I followed her to the den where she was sitting on the floor, searching through an old photo box. "Here it is," she said, handing it to me. It was a photo, carefully protected in a clear plastic sleeve, a black and white photo of a baby in a *tzute*, the sling Guatemalan mothers used to carry their babies, two rectangular breadths of fabric sewn together to form a square.

The photo looked familiar. "It's you," Leah said. "The first photo the adoption agency in Guatemala sent us . . . of you."

I looked at it closely. It was a small photo, only three inches by three inches, like a passport photo, but the image was sharp and perfectly centered.

"Don't you think it belongs . . . in your collage?" Leah asked, looking up at me with a hopeful smile.

I looked at her and remembered the expensive office tie she'd bought for Miles the day after he was laid off from Boeing. No matter how hard I'd tried to fight it,

Leah's hopefulness had always been contagious, and I felt it wrap around me like an old blanket.

"You're right, Mom. It's perfect."

After I was done, Bryn helped me wrap up the collage in bubble wrap and put it in the trunk of my car. Bryn closed her eyes and took my hand. *"Qisma,"* Bryn pronounced, like an incantation into the dusk, then gently pushed the top of the trunk down. By the time I arrived at Jack's house, it was dark outside. Bryn waited in the car while I walked up to the door.

The porch light was out, and the house looked deserted, but through the window, I could see Aiden sitting at the desk in the living room. The room was dark too, except for the three computer screens, lit up, Aiden in silhouette. All three screens were going at the same time, each one with different images. The first was a time lapse of the ocean and the sun streaking across the sky. The second was a blur of water against metal. Last was the arc of a whale rising from the water, like an island erupting from the bottom of the ocean. I stood there for a few minutes, unable to move, watching him combine the images, mix them and transform them. His hands flew furiously over the keyboard, and he leaned so far into the screens I thought they would swallow him up.

Slowly, I set my package down on the doorstep.

And with the package, I left a little note. It had taken me weeks to find the right words in the book. They'd been buried deep inside Chapter 115. They were nine hopeful words. And with those nine words, I added three of my own.

"Set all sail and keep her to the wind."
Keep her.

—*Maddie*

It was after midnight when I came back to the house. I headed to the laundry room and fished out Bryn's pomegranate T-shirt from the Goodwill bag. I put it on the kitchen table, fired up Leah's iron, and ironed out all the wrinkles.

January 15, 2008

Dear Alex—

We're heading back, our fuel almost gone. And that's how I feel, spent and done, with the sky, with the ocean, and with the wind. We've chased away one whaling ship across five thousand miles of ocean. But there will be others, other killing ships. They won't stop.

The footage I took is probably no good, but it doesn't matter. I know that making a film was just something I could hide behind through all this.

I can still see you in your room doing homework, and in the backyard painting your protest signs. I see you with your book, reading near the bay window. And even though it's been more than three thousand days since the accident, I still miss you every day, every minute.

I go over it and over it again and again, that day, like a video on a continuous loop, and I wish I could just erase it and start over, but I can't.

I wish Jack's plane from Boston hadn't been delayed, and we would have all gone to the airport to pick him up as Mom had planned. I wish it hadn't been summer, those long days of sunlight. Then maybe you wouldn't have taken your bike out to the street. I wish I'd paid attention to the sound of the front door as it closed when you left the house to ride. I wish that driver had stopped.

You were only twelve, but you were already an old soul and you were always in a hurry. You were so anxious to finish things, to make them happen. You always worried about leaving something behind, and we all used

to laugh that you were too young to be concerned about
something like that, but we were all wrong. You knew
your time was short, and you were in a hurry, even to
ride your new bike.

This is what you left behind, Alex. This voyage on the
Esperanza, on a ship named "Hope," and the almost one
hundred whales we saved on this trip. You did this.

I'm not really sure of my plans. When we return to
Auckland, I think I'll stay for a few months in New Zealand,
maybe help train new volunteers then fly back to California
to see Mom and Dad. Maybe I'll stay there for a while and
work on the footage with Jack in Los Angeles. He would
know if there's anything worth salvaging into a film.

I'm packing up my clothes and gear when Olivia
appears at my berth.

"I saw it in my Tarot cards," Olivia says to me, and I
start to laugh, but she's completely serious this time.

"I saw you with a girl," she says, and I'm still packing
and half-listening.

"You, right?"

"No. Not me. Someone else. It was the Empress
card," she says.

I try to remember what the Empress looks like. She's
the queen of heaven, dark-haired and has a crown of stars.
Pomegranates decorate her long gown, and she sits in a
forest of trees and grass, holding a staff beneath a yellow
sky. I vaguely remember Olivia's theatrical explanations in
the mess. She gives and nurtures life.

"Oh, sure. She's a life force. She's Mother Nature," I
say, in my most exaggerated voice.

But Olivia isn't laughing.

"She gives birth to art," Olivia says.

"Come on, Olivia," I say to her. "Give me a break. You don't really believe in all that."

"I do," she says, and I go on packing.

"Pomegranates," she continues. "You'll know for sure when you see the pomegranates."

"Pomegranates? Now you're being completely ridiculous, Olivia," I say.

She waits a minute.

"Please stop packing, Aiden. There's also something else. A child," Olivia says, and I stop. Olivia's expression is completely calm, but more than that, intoxicating. I look at her face and there's something very different about her. It's the look of someone who is giving me a gift.

"Keep a watch out for a queen," she says, "for the one who wears pomegranates. Promise?"

It's the longing in her voice that makes me give her my pledge. I recognize it so well, the ache to repair and to reinvent. After all, there can't be any harm in this promise, because there's no chance, not even a chance in a million that something like that could ever happen.

Al – ways –

Aiden

CHAPTER 38

THE HEAT FINALLY BROKE IN MID-OCTOBER. I'D said my good-byes to Bryn and Angela, Uncle Phil and Adele, and left a voicemail for Jack. I was all packed, my housing assignment and the student loan paperwork carefully folded up in my carryon bag. Jorge had reserved a redeye for me out of LAX, and we were all in the car—Leah, Miles, Jorge, and Gabby. But traffic was unusually light and everyone wanted to stop at Randy's donut place on the way. When we got there, I got out of the car and took a photograph of the giant, thirty-two foot concrete donut sitting on its roof, then went inside with Jorge and ordered a mixed dozen. It was twilight, and just outside the donut shop an amateur astronomer had set up a twelve-inch reflector telescope on the sidewalk. His handwritten sign said "urban guerilla astronomy," and he was stopping people who were walking by, trying to entice them to look through his telescope.

"You can see the craters of the moon, the moons of Jupiter or the rings of Saturn," the amateur astronomer called out. Curious, I watched as one person took him up on his offer and put his eye gingerly against the lens.

"How about you?" the amateur astronomer turned to me.

"No thanks."

"Are you sure?"

I looked up at the clear night sky, and felt myself yielding to its pull. I rested one eye on the eyepiece, closing the other, and let the telescope gather up light and mirrors, and I could see the moon below the Maiden, Saturn in her arms, and the Great Bear and Little Bear playing beneath the North Queen.

Yesterday, I'd opened the envelope Aiden had given me. Inside, were the letters he'd written to Alex. Each one was handwritten on different pieces of paper. There were torn-out film production sheets, sea log journals, the backs of envelopes and napkins, lined and unlined paper. I read each one over and over again, taking in their colors.

Inky blue, deck green, and Tarot card red.

Each one of them was a piece of a collage named Aiden.

It had been weeks since I'd heard from him, and I was certain he'd signed off on the adoption papers. Outside, the sky was turning a deeper blue-black, as if it agreed with me.

Jorge came out with a box full of donuts and handed it through the car window to Gabriela. "Let's do a *force* Mads," and I knew what he meant. Every time we'd taken a family trip and stopped off at a landmark, Jorge would position himself, stretching his right hand out, cupped, as though he was holding the landmark up, and then ask me to take a photo. It was called forced perspective, a photographic trick. Unlike human eyes, which worked together to create depth perception, the camera only had one eye.

There were dozens of these photos at home, Jorge holding up City Hall, Hoover Dam, and the Golden Gate Bridge. It wasn't a difficult photo to take. It was all about the two of us standing in the right spots, his hand and the landmark in the right perspective through my lens. "C'mon," he said, when he saw I was resisting, and I happily relented.

Back in the car, the donuts were good. I ate two, sugary and sticky, and Miles headed back on the road to the horseshoe-shaped airport. Miles's old office wasn't far away, only a few miles farther south, and I remembered the times Miles had taken us to Parking Lot C, the lot that sat directly under the approach path, where we could feel and hear the thunder of the planes as they landed so close above us.

At the departures curb, I said my good-byes to everyone, hugging Leah first, then handing her a letter. "Mail this for me, Mom?"

Leah turned over the envelope, and tears welled up in her eyes. The letter was addressed to Alma and Raphael in Guatemala, and I'd already affixed the postage. "You were right, Mom, as usual. It was good for me."

I hugged Gabriela and finally Jorge, but as Miles shut the trunk, he took me aside.

"After you land at JFK, don't forget to take photographs of the old TWA building," Miles said. "It's still there, right near the Jet Blue terminal."

"The bird building?"

"Yes, that's it." Miles had often talked about it, the tube-like flight wing walkways inside the bird-shaped building designed in the sixties.

"I used to go through there a lot when I worked for Boeing," Miles said. "I loved getting off the red-eye and seeing it at sunrise. So take lots of photos for me." I looked at him, and I could have sworn I smelled something along with the jet fuel in the air. It was the faint smell of rain. I hugged my dad and rolled my carryon bag inside the terminal and up through security to the last gate.

Beyond the floor-to-ceiling windows was the space-age restaurant, sitting on spidery legs. Nearby, the Los Angeles River emptied out to the Pacific Ocean. After six rainless months, the river was nothing but a dried-out riverbed, but soon it wouldn't be. I could see the rain falling lightly on the tarmac, and I could imagine the rush of water that would soon course through it, water born in the mountains and glaciers up north. The water would head down, through the concrete channels of the river on its way to spill out into the ocean.

I took out my camera and looked at the last photo I'd taken—Jorge holding up a giant donut in the palm of his hand, and I laughed out loud. The enormous donut was perfectly balanced in the palm of Jorge's hand, securely there and left behind, in the photo, forever.

Soon people got up from their seats and started to line up to board the plane. I was last to leave my seat, and fell in at the very end of the line. I was just about to turn off my phone when it lit up and rang. It was Aiden. And along with him, the noise of the city in motion, taxi cabs honking, and a lone siren. He was in New York.

But then I heard the tiniest of sounds.

It was the voice of a baby named Hope.

MORE

Want to know more about Maddie and Aiden?

There's more at <u>www.leorakrygier.net</u> *where you can—*

- See Maddie's photos and the actual places you read about in *Keep Her*

- Follow Maddie and Aiden's journey on Google Maps

- See the handwritten letters Aiden wrote to Alex

- Take Action! — find links to great organizations

- See the Southern Ocean whale migration maps

- Watch the real *Esperanza*'s ship's web cam

- Find links to tips, contests, and other great stuff for writers and photographers

Also—

Instagram: @leorakrygierauthor

Twitter: @leorakrygier

ACKNOWLEDGMENTS

There are so many people to thank and to acknowledge.

I start with my family, whose love and support always help to clear the thorny path—my husband, David; my children Talia and Oren, and their spouses, Israel and Lindsay; my brothers, Ron and Zach; my sisters, Dena, Karen, Irit, and Rachel; my one and only cousin, Daphna; my second mom, Edith; my second family, the Altits; and my parents, Yael and Levi.

And my devoted friends—too many to name, but I will try. My high school BFF's, Ivy and Diane; and Saralyn, Randi, Lucy, Joya, Lisya, Debbie, Nardit, Marlene, Ruti, Rivi, Rene, Cathi, Paulette, and Babs.

Can't forget my loving writing, author buddies and cheerleaders—Carolyn Howard Johnson, Bob Stone, Jackie Hirtz, Linda Schreyer, Sarah Lamstein, Agatha Dominick, Kenn Heller, and Marion Rosenberg—who brainstorm, plow through drafts, copy edit, and put up with most of my whining.

And to Brooke Warner and Cait Levin of She Writes Press, who have created a beautiful, nurturing home for books.

Just one more, thanks to Kobi, my first dog—so loyal and true, and very wise—who taught me to respect and protect all our animals and planet Earth.

ABOUT THE AUTHOR

LEORA KRYGIER is the author of *When She Sleeps* (Toby Press) a New York Public Library Selection for "Best Books for the Teen Age," and about which *Newsweek* raved, "Krygier's luminous prose transports the reader." She is also a former Los Angeles Superior Court judge and the author of *Juvenile Court: A Judge's Guide for Young Adults and their Parents* (Scarecrow Press). She lives in Los Angeles with her husband. When she's not writing, she loves to go to the beach, walk the Santa Monica Mountain trails, and snap lots and lots of photographs.

SELECTED TITLES FROM SHE WRITES PRESS

She Writes Press is an independent publishing company
founded to serve women writers everywhere.
Visit us at www.shewritespress.com.

The Lucidity Project by Abbey Campbell Cook. $16.95, 978-1-63152-032-7. After suffering from depression all her life, twenty-five-year-old Max Dorigan joins a mysterious research project on a Caribbean island, where she's introduced to the magical and healing world of lucid dreaming.

Beautiful Garbage by Jill DiDonato. $16.95, 978-1-938314-01-8. Talented but troubled young artist Jodi Plum leaves suburbia for the excitement of the city—and is soon swept up in the sexual politics and downtown art scene of 1980s New York.

Cleans Up Nicely by Linda Dahl. $16.95, 978-1-938314-38-4. The story of one gifted young woman's path from self-destruction to self-knowledge, set in mid-1970s Manhattan.

Fire & Water by Betsy Graziani Fasbinder. $16.95, 978-1-938314-14-8. Kate Murphy has always played by the rules—but when she meets charismatic artist Jake Bloom, she's forced to navigate the treacherous territory of passionate love, friendship, and family devotion.

A Drop in the Ocean: A Novel by Jenni Ogden. $16.95, 978-1-63152-026-6. When middle-aged Anna Fergusson's research lab is abruptly closed, she flees Boston to an island on Australia's Great Barrier Reef—where, amongst the seabirds, nesting turtles, and eccentric islanders, she finds a family and learns some bittersweet lessons about love.

The Wiregrass by Pam Webber. $16.95, 978-1-63152-943-6. A story about a summer of discontent, change, and dangerous mysteries in a small Southern Wiregrass town.